Private
Investigation

The Billionaires' Club Series: Book 10

AE Moran

The Invisible Publishing Company

The Billionaires' Club Series

Book 1: Hostile Takeover

Book 2: Cruel Obsession

Book 3: Enemy Betrothed

Book 4: Rising Star

Book 5: Forever Young

Book 6: Broken Idol

Book 7: Last Hope

Book 8: New Blood

Book 9: Falsely Accused

Book 10: Private Investigation

Contents

Chapter 1: Rory   1

Chapter 2: Nicole   11

Chapter 3: Nicole   21

Chapter 4: Rory   29

Chapter 5: Nicole   35

Chapter 6: Nicole   41

Chapter 7: Rory   49

Chapter 8: Nicole   55

Chapter 9: Nicole   65

Chapter 10: Rory   73

Chapter 11: Rory   79

Chapter 12: Nicole   85

Chapter 13: Nicole   91

Chapter 14: Nicole   97

Chapter 15: Nicole   103

Chapter 16: Rory   113

Chapter 17: Rory   119

Chapter 18: Rory   125

Chapter 19: Rory   131

Chapter 20: Nicole   139

Chapter 21: Rory   147

Chapter 22: Nicole   153

Chapter 23: Nicole   159

Chapter 24: Rory   167

Chapter 25: Rory   175

Chapter 26: Nicole   183

Chapter 27: Nicole   199

Chapter 28: Nicole   205

Chapter 29: Rory   211

Chapter 30: Nicole   219

Chapter 31: Rory   227

Chapter 32: Rory   235

Chapter 33: Nicole   243

Chapter 34: Nicole   249

Keep Reading   265

Get All of AE Moran's Free Books   267

About AE Moran   269

Also by AE Moran (so far)   271

Chapter 1: Rory

"There he is! The man of the hour!" Niko Holloway holds out his hand to shake mine.

I laugh at him. "I'm not the man of the hour. You are."

"Why am I the man of the hour? You're the bigshot club officer. I'm nobody."

I laugh again and feel my cheeks burning. "You could be an officer if you wanted to be. You're every bit as good as I am. I'm only the club's PR officer because I work in PR."

He flushes the same way. He won't stop grinning. "I don't have any skills the club needs."

"Don't lie. Every man here wants to do business with you."

"Every man here does do business with *you*," he returns and we both laugh.

We both turn to look around The Billionaires' Club. We're the youngest men in the room and in the whole club. The only other member close to our age is Giovanni Nowaczyk and he isn't here right now.

He's a year older than I am and Niko is six months younger. Giovanni spends a lot more time with the older billionaires since he got married and settled down.

He never spent too much time with Niko and me before Giovanni got married, either. He was too busy playing the field with any girl with a pulse. He could get as many girls as he wanted anytime he wanted and he took full advantage of that.

Niko and I have always been much more serious. Niko was a hardcore businessman dedicated to his craft long before he got married. Getting married didn't change that about him.

He and I have always had that in common. We've been friends for years and him getting married didn't change that, either.

"How's your wife doing?" I ask. "Why isn't she here? She always used to come to club meetings."

"She's been practically bedridden with crippling nausea since she got pregnant. She's barely gotten out of bed since we got the positive test result. She runs her companies from her phone and computer."

"At least it's temporary, right? I mean….she has to give birth sometime, right?"

He gives me a look. "She better."

I laugh, and right then, Kevin Drake steps out of the cluster of men he's talking to. He waves me toward him. "Are you coming?" I ask Niko.

"You go ahead. I'm hungry. I want to get something to eat. I'll catch up with you later."

"Tell Melody to call me, okay? I need to get her input on that prosecution case in Rome."

"Yeah, sure," he replies over his shoulder. "I'll tell her."

I cross the club and join up with Kevin. He's talking to Derek Salazar and Judah Hayes. "Just the man we wanted to see," Derek tells me.

"What's up?"

"Derek and Judah want to start a new venture together," Kevin tells me. "They need you to handle publicity."

"What's the venture?" I ask. "Let me guess. It's something financial services related."

Derek and Judah both grin. "You're a regular clairvoyant, aren't you?" Derek teases.

"I was just suggesting that they should ask you...." Kevin begins, but right then, one of the security guards comes into the club from downstairs. He's a heavy-set black guy of twenty-five named Donny.

"Excuse me, Mr. Kahn," he tells me. "There's a reporter outside trying to get in and question everyone."

"Tell him we don't address the press at club meetings," Kevin replies over his shoulder. "Tell him to contact Rory through the club's website contact page."

"Excuse me, Mr. Drake, but she's a woman and we already tried to tell her that," Donny counters. "She refuses to leave until she talks to someone who is actually in the club."

"I'll handle this." I turn back to Kevin and the others. "You fellas go on with your meeting. I'll get rid of her."

"I'll come with you," Kevin tells me. "We'll be able to body-slam her to the ground if she turns psycho."

I laugh and we follow Donny downstairs. We find the other two guards, Frank and Ricky, facing off against a youngish woman of about thirty. She wears her wavy blonde hair down to her shoulders and tinted pale rose pink at the ends.

She's wearing a white pencil skirt, matching blazer, and a pea-cock-blue blouse underneath with glaring, Day-Glo pink pumps. Her handbag is more of a fuchsia pink.

She has an expensive, glamorous style that makes her delicate, youthful features look extremely pretty. She looks just pretty, glamorous, and expensive enough to think she can probably get away with shit like this because of her looks.

"Can I help you, Ma'am?" I asked her.

She takes one look at me, blinks, and then glances at Kevin. "My name is Nicole Bates." She holds out her hand to each of us one after another. "I work for the *New York Record*. It's a news outlet dedicated to commercial, financial, and political interests. I would like to meet with your organization and interview the membership about certain high-profile incidents that have come to light recently."

"I know what the *New York Record* is, Ms. Bates," Kevin tells her. "Club meetings are private and not open to the public. This is Rory Kahn. He's our PR officer. You can contact him through the club's website contact page—or you can interview the members elsewhere. I'll have to ask you to leave."

"Wait a minute, Kevin," I tell him and turn to her. "What incidents did you want to ask us about?"

She looks back and forth between us and then confronts Kevin. "You're Kevin Drake—CEO of People, Inc.? You're the club's membership officer, aren't you? You're in charge of new members who apply and join the club. Isn't that right?"

"Yes, that's correct. Don't tell me you want to join the club."

"Of course not. I'm not a billionaire." She makes a face when she says it. "Is it true that you met your wife, Paige Novak, when she applied for membership in the club—and actually when she had only been in New York for a matter of days?"

"Actually she only inquired about applying for membership. She hadn't actually applied yet—but yes, it's true that she came to the club within days of moving to New York," Kevin replies. "That is when I met her."

"Did you use your position as membership officer to go out with her?" Nicole asks.

"Of course not!" Kevin counters. "She was married to someone else at the time. Our interaction was strictly professional."

"Did you use your position to break up her marriage?" she asks.

"NO!!" he screams. "It was never like that! How can you even insinuate that?!"

I step in again and hold out my hand to her. "I'll handle this, Kevin. Go back inside."

He glares at her and then at me.

"Go, Kevin. I'll deal with this."

He compresses his lips and storms up the stairs. I can't think of any subject more likely to piss him off than to suggest that he did something underhanded to get with his wife. He's already touchy enough about the subject.

He's such a friendly, outgoing, laid-back guy normally. It takes a lot to set him off, but I can see this reporter trying to get there just as soon as she possibly can.

She turns her beady eyes on me next. I sense Donny, Ricky, and Frank all standing behind me watching and listening to every word.

I wave her forward. "Come on upstairs," I tell her. "I'll show you around."

She furrows her brow. "Is this some kind of trick? He just said I'm not allowed inside."

"You can come inside because I'm going to escort you around. I'll answer your questions and you can see what it's like. You won't be able to question the other members. I can give you whatever information you want."

She narrows her eyes at me. "What's the catch?"

"There is no catch except that you won't get to interview anyone but me. The club has nothing to hide, but you have to understand that this is a private get-together among friends. This isn't a press conference. No one came here to get interviewed by a reporter. You can do that on your own time after you go to the trouble of contacting each of them and getting their consent."

She scrutinizes me a little longer. She's pretty, but I don't see anything exceptional about her in the looks department. She just knows how to dress and she has nice style.

Maybe she'll be happy with a brief explanation of what she wants to know. Then she'll disappear just like all the other reporters who get the idea to look into the club.

She finally compresses her lips and follows me to the building entrance. I escort her upstairs. The other guys glance over at her and go back to their conversations as if Nicole isn't here.

I show her around the main room, the office, and a few other places. The tour doesn't tell her anything. The club is just another building.

"Are your meetings only for men?" she asks once we get upstairs. "Why aren't any of your female club members here?"

"We have four female members on our roster at the moment. They all have businesses to run and Melody Gottlieb is sick in bed with pregnancy nausea. Any of the members can come or not come to these weekly get-togethers. Quite a few of the male club members aren't here, either. People have things to do. It's up to them if they come or n ot."

"Who are the other officers?"

I point across the room. "Judah Hayes is our events officer. He's the only other officer here besides me and Kevin. Dante Helme is our president. Jackson Metcalf is our finance officer. Lane Prince is our property officer."

She makes a face at me. "Don't you think it's a little suspicious that each of these officers has been involved in some high-profile scandal directly related to the club? It looks an awful lot like these officers are predatory and use their positions to get what they want—especially with women."

"What do you mean?"

"Kevin Drake used his position as membership officer to get in bed with one of the very few female billionaires to walk through that door. He acted as a gatekeeper and pressured her to get with him so she could gain access to the club."

I snort at her. "Who told you that? It didn't happen like that at all. I don't know who told you that, but whoever it is doesn't know what they're talking about."

"It isn't just him. Niko Holloway took advantage of Melody Gottlieb and manipulated her into a marriage she didn't want to get his hands on her father's fortune. Dante Helme used his authority to manipulate a much younger woman into a predatory relationship with him."

I shake my head and look away. "You don't know anything about these people. It's obvious you haven't done even the smallest amount of research to find out what really happened. Who told you this stuff, anyway?"

"If that's not what happened, what did?"

I take a minute to decide how to answer her.

"You see?" she snaps. "You know it's true. You can't justify these men acting like predators on any woman who comes near the club."

"I can justify it because they aren't predators and they didn't manipulate anyone. Melody's father Saul was the one who pressured her into a marriage she didn't want. Niko didn't want to marry Melody at all. Saul was the one who made the marriage a condition of a business deal between him, Dante, and Niko—and Niko has never gotten a penny of Saul's money since Melody inherited her father's empire."

"I don't believe you."

"Have you interviewed Melody about this? Have you even asked her about the circumstances that led to her marrying Niko? Every single company in Melody's organization is held independently and legally insulated from Niko's—and he was the one who set it up that way. He and Melody worked together as a couple to keep his business separate from hers. They don't cross over at all. He isn't involved in her companies and he never gets any money from them. They're married because they love each other. He offered to dissolve the marriage after her father's death because he thought she would want to keep it separate. He never wanted to take advantage of her. He loves her more than anything."

"You're lying. You would say anything to defend your friend."

"It sounds to me like you haven't even done the bare minimum of investigation into this story. You plan to publish whatever slanderous smear campaign you can come up with and the facts be damned. Did you know that Dante was mentoring Emberlynn in business when she came up with the whole concept for the MegaDome Experience? He was the one who supported her to build her empire—and that was before they ever went out on their first date. He helped her get started. He mentored her, coached her, encouraged her, and introduced her to her first investors in the club. He wasn't going out with her at the time. She applied for a job at one of his companies and she didn't get it because he recused himself from the hiring process to keep it impartial. They weren't involved then, either. Their relationship developed afterward. Kevin and Paige partnered in business while she was still married to her first husband. Their interaction was strictly professional until after Paige and Trent finalized their divorce. Kevin actively distanced himself from her until long after she had been a member of the club in good standing for months. There was never anything predatory, manipulative, or inappropriate about any of their relationships—and there still isn't. You can research them until the cows come home. You won't find anything untoward because there isn't anything untoward to find."

She sniffs at me and looks away. "That isn't what I heard."

"Why don't you interview the women involved? Why are you even here if you don't have even that small level of journalistic integrity?"

She spins around fast and narrows her eyes at me. "Are you questioning my journalistic integrity?"

"Have you interviewed the women involved? If they don't think their husbands acted inappropriately, why should you or anyone else?"

"Oh, I plan to interview the women involved. Giovanni Nowaczyk used his money and influence to weasel himself into a blind woman's life when she was vulnerable and couldn't take care of herself—and Diego Espinosa got arrested for violently murdering his business partner. What kind of organization are you even running here?"

I can only shake my head in amazement. "Wow, lady. You really got it bad, don't you? You really need to do your homework before you go out in public throwing accusations like that around."

"I don't hear you defending them."

"For one thing, the charges against Diego Espinosa were dropped shortly after his arrest—which was politically motivated, I should add. The real killer is currently serving a life sentence in Riker's Island—and Mila Knapp went blind *after* she had already married Giovanni. They were an established couple long before she went blind. She wasn't vulnerable. She had a thriving career as a photographer and he definitely didn't weasel his way into her life. He has a disability and she has a disability. They help each other and they have a beautiful family anyone would envy and be proud of. They all do. I honestly don't see how you or anyone else can find out anything about them and think these men would ever do anything to undermine or prey on their wives. They're the most upstanding men I've ever met—and their wives are the happiest, most successful women I've ever met." I frown at her. "Have you ever even met these women? Have you ever seen any of them in public?"

She looks away, so that answers my question.

Kevin comes back over to us just then. "Is everything under control?"

"Everything is fine," I tell him. "Ms. Bates was just leaving."

"That's good because the meeting will be ending in ten minutes." He turns to Nicole. "Today will be the exception, Ms. Bates. You won't be allowed back inside the club again. You'll have to get your material another way."

"I plan to. Thank you for your time."

She walks out of the club by herself.

Chapter 2: Nicole

I pull up my laptop and find a comfortable position on the couch to do some research on my latest news article. I already have the perfect title picked out, *There's No Such Thing As a Good Billionaire.* That should grab a few eyeballs.

First I do a search on Rory Kahn. He's the club's PR officer. He's probably the biggest snake in the nest.

Everybody knows what a player Giovanni Nowaczyk was in his early days before he married Mila Knapp. His exploits are the stuff of legend, but he isn't the only one.

He, Rory, and Niko Holloway are the youngest club members and Rory is the only one of the three who isn't married.

The word on the street is that Giovanni settled down after he got married, but that could just be the club putting a spin on what's really going on behind the scenes.

He could be getting his wife to say all kinds of things to make him look better—especially if he manipulated her at the beginning.

Rory seems like the King of Spin. He certainly talked a good game when I met him at the club. He said all the right things in all the right places, but that doesn't mean he was telling the truth.

He's a spin doctor. Why wouldn't he do the same thing for the club's public image?

He certainly looks the part. He's five-foot-seven, immaculately dressed, and stunningly good-looking with the back of his dark brown hair buzzed high up his neck and the top cut long and swept sideways. He certainly knows how to make himself look good.

I find a ton of other information on him. Plenty of periodicals and other news outlets have done spotlight pieces on him. These outlets do spot pieces on all the billionaires.

There are a lot more spots about him than the other billionaires because of where he comes from. He ran away from an abusive foster home in Pittsburgh when he was eight.

He lived on the street, hid from the authorities, and survived out of dumpsters until he graduated from high school. The foster parents never reported him missing because they were worried he might snitch on them.

He worked two jobs to put himself through community college. The first job was as a graveyard-shift janitor at a PR firm in Brooklyn. He paid attention and learned the PR business there.

His other job was as a dishwasher in the kitchen at a different local high school. He got fired from the job because he got caught passing extra food to other homeless and abused kids who came to school hungry.

A reporter found out about the story and caused a massive public outcry that led to the school district starting a free meals for kids program for anyone who didn't get enough at home.

The program didn't help Rory. He got another job working as a nighttime cleaner at one of Holden Seager's companies.

While he was there, Rory noticed a PR campaign another agency was doing for the company. Rory approached Holden, pointed out a bunch of things wrong with the campaign, and offered to do it right for half the price.

That was Rory's first paid PR contract and it launched the company that later made him a billionaire. He doesn't have a reputation as a player.

In fact, not a single reporter has been able to uncover even one person, male or female, who claims they've been in a relationship with him or ever even slept with him. He's been alone all his adult life—or else he's just extremely discreet.

It's an amazing story—even more amazing than some of the rags-to-riches stories the other billionaires in the club can tell. It's pretty amazing that someone can have worked so hard and come so far.

It's strange that he doesn't do more to enjoy his wealth. He doesn't live in a lavish penthouse apartment or a giant estate like some of the others. He lives in a modest, middle-class apartment on the Upper West Side.

The only difference is that he owns the building. A manager deals with all the tenants.

I get a phone call from my editor just then. "Where's the piece you were supposed to do on The Billionaires' Club?" he asks.

"You said I had until Friday to turn it in. I haven't had a chance to interview anyone. They stonewalled me at the club. I have to go around interviewing everyone separately. That will take time."

"We're bumping up your timeline. Just send it in so we can run it."

"I won't be able to interview anyone if I do that."

"Don't worry about it. We need the piece for the lifestyle page. You can get the quotes and personal details right in a follow-up piece if you have to."

We get off the phone and I start typing out the story I've been formulating in my head. I include all the incidents of manipulative, predatory, misogynistic behavior I mentioned at the club.

I do the final proofread on the article and attach it to my editor's email address. I hesitate with my finger poised over the mouse before I hit *Send*.

Rory's words ring in my ear. Journalistic integrity.

No one has ever questioned my journalistic integrity before. I consider that the worst insult anyone can level at me.....but he's right. Publishing this piece is wrong. My gut tells me so, but I can't do anything about that.

I hit *Send* and get busy arranging all my interviews. I get appointments with the most high-profile women associated with the club. Some of them are easy. I start with Melody Gottlieb. She's famous.

I have a harder time getting an appointment with Paige Novak. She's too busy and her assistant tells me he'll have to check with her to find out when she'll be available.

I find it much easier to get an appointment with Vivian Salazar, Derek Salazar's wife. She's a stay-at-home mother. Of course a rich guy like that would keep his wife tied to the stove by her apron strings.

Then I do some digging into the murder rap against Diego Espinosa. The detective who investigated the charge against him is a certain Jocelyn Hitchcock. She's retired from the Force after getting shot in the line of duty.

I look up her contact information and frown at the screen. She has the same mailing address as Diego. What does that mean?

I don't think too much about it. I leave the house the next morning and drive across town to a giant high-rise building where I ride up to an equally luxurious penthouse apartment.

A haggard woman in a grubby, faded, dark blue terrycloth bathrobe opens the door. She looks extremely hungover with dark bags under her eyes, creases across her face, and her auburn hair going in every direction.

She's wearing a pair of rumpled flannel pajamas under her robe, fuzzy slippers, and she isn't wearing a bra under her pajama top.

"Um....excuse me...." I stammer. "I have an appointment to interview Melody Gottlieb. Is she home?"

The woman stands aside and waves at nothing. "You might as well come inside," she grumbles in a congested undertone.

I take a step across the threshold. The apartment is enormous and perfectly clean and presentable. She's the only person here. I don't see the billionaire female CEO I'm supposed to interview.

"Will Ms. Gottlieb be here soon?" I ask.

The woman goes into the living room, throws herself down on the couch, tosses her arm over her face, and growls at me from under the sleeve of her robe. "Ms. Gottlieb has left the building, Ms. Bates. Whatever you want to ask me, you better go ahead and get it over with. You'll have to forgive me if I don't sit up and...."

She shoots off the couch, sprints to a nearby hall, throws open the door to a bathroom, and pukes into the toilet.

Rory's comments drift back into my brain. *Melody Gottlieb is suffering from pregnancy nausea.* This is her. This is the bigshot billionaire female CEO I'm supposed to interview.

I stand in one spot and stare at her. The puking sounds coming from the bathroom go on for a long time. No wonder she looks so awful.

She eventually spits, rinses her mouth out in the sink, blows her nose, and groans again. She shuffles around the apartment for a while and comes back into the living room carrying a plastic bucket and her cellphone.

She takes up residence in the same place on the couch, puts her bucket on the floor right next to her head, and shoots me a withering glare. "You're the one who wanted to talk to me. This wasn't my idea."

I clear my throat and sit down on one of the armchairs across from her. "Sorry. I wouldn't have disturbed you if I had known you were in such bad shape."

"Oh, I'm in great shape. That's the problem," she mutters. "The doctors say this is a sign of a healthy pregnancy. Can you believe that? I'm supposed to be happy about this, so you better be, too." She collapses back on the cushions. "What did you want to ask me about?"

"I'm doing an article on predatory behavior by some of the male members of The Billionaires' Club toward women who are either financially vulnerable or in subordinate positions where the men can use their power, money, and influence to get what they want. I understand Niko Holloway pursued an arranged marriage with you for financial gain."

She snorts. "Niko never pursued anything with me. The marriage idea was the absolute last thing in the world that he wanted. Trust me, Ms. Bates. Niko never stood to benefit from this marriage at all."

"Then.....why did he enter it if he was so opposed to it?"

"He entered it because Dante Helme wanted to use this marriage as a bridge between Niko and my father. They held a grudge against each other. The marriage was the only way they could get into business with each other with Dante acting as the middleman."

"Then Niko did stand to gain from the marriage."

"Niko stood to gain from the deal, but he could have done the deal without the marriage. My father was the one who really pushed the marriage through. It was Dante's idea, but I only went along with it because my father was desperate. He would have been ruined if not for that deal. That's why I did it. Niko had nothing to do with it."

"Rory Kahn says Niko offered to dissolve the marriage when you inherited your father's fortune. Is that true?"

"Niko offered to dissolve the marriage many times. He was the only person involved in the deal who understood how bad it was for me. He never wanted that for me."

My head shoots up. "Are you serious?"

She sees exactly what's going through my mind. She makes a face at me. "Niko Holloway was the best thing that has ever happened to me. He was unbelievably kind and understanding about the whole thing. He made it tolerable when it wasn't. He saved my life—literally. Everything I have I owe to Niko. He took a nightmare scenario and turned it into the life of my dreams. I would gladly give up my entire fortune to live in a paper bag with him. He never manipulated me or preyed on me or anything like that. Everyone else did that. He was the one who saved me from it—not the other way around." She snorts again, turns over onto her back, and throws her arm over her face again. "I don't know where you're getting your information. It sounds like someone has been drinking the Kool-Aid on the side."

I blink at the side of her face. I have a hard time believing what she's saying—but I can't believe she's some kind of cringing doormat or abused woman who is repeating what her asshole husband told her to say to defend his reputation.

Melody's reputation as a hardcore businesswoman is second to none in business circles. She's known for being on top of everything and turning most of her father's companies from close to bankruptcy to thriving, growing, and booming.

I haven't been able to find a single complaint against Niko Holloway, either. He's always been considered a sharp, savvy, scrupulous businessman with unquestioned integrity and a strict work ethic.

I'm going to have to do a little more digging into the details of their arranged marriage. Those words alone sound so disgusting and predatory. *Arranged marriage.* Who even does that in this day and age?

"Is it true that you and Niko keep your finances separated?" I ask. "Some people at the club think all of your business dealings are insulated from each other."

"All my father's assets were tied up before the wedding in corporate structures and trust instruments—and Niko did the same thing. Neither Niko nor my father trusted each other to save their own lives. They both protected themselves down to the ground, so there was nothing to separate after my father died. The only question was whether we would stay together or not after we no longer needed the marriage to keep the deal going."

"And you obviously decided to stay together. Was that your choice or his?"

"I just told you. He offered to dissolve the marriage because he was the one who said he didn't want to make any claim on my fortune. I insisted that we stay together because we loved each other. I didn't want to do it without him. He was my primary support. He was the one who got me through it. He taught me more about business than I could have learned on my own. He's the only reason I am where I am today. He's guided me, mentored me, supported me, and encouraged me every step of the way. There is no one in the world more committed to my success than Niko is." She sneers at me. "He never needed my money. He was never interested in my money. He cares too much about earning it himself. He doesn't want to steal it."

"I....uh...." I pretend to look at my phone. "I think I better go. Thank you so much for your time. I really hope you feel better soon....."

"So do I," she mutters.

I get out of the apartment as quickly as I can. Something is seriously wrong with this story. What if she's right and someone has been telling me a bunch of lies about what these people are all about?

Chapter 3: Nicole

I squint through the cab window and check the address on my phone. "Are you sure this is the right place?"

"You're the one who gave me the address, lady," the cab driver growls over his shoulder. "If it ain't the right place, that's your fault."

I pay the fare and get out of the cab. He drives off and leaves me standing there. I turn around and stare at the house in the distance.

It doesn't look like a billionaire's house at all. It looks like a normal family home surrounded by gardens, fruit trees, and a few animals grazing behind fences.

Flowers grow in beds by the door and line each walkway. The whole scene looks like something out of a children's book. A long driveway curves from the house out to the road where I stand staring.

The front door of the house bursts open just then and two young children charge outside. They run around on the grass yelling their heads off while a woman watches them from the porch. This is the most idyllic scene imaginable.

No one would ever guess this place was still in New York. Derek and Vivian Salazar live in a rural part of Long Island away from noise, crowds, and traffic.

I don't know what to think. This definitely isn't what I pictured when I made the appointment to interview Vivian, but I don't want to go all the way back to Manhattan empty-handed.

I set off trekking up the driveway. My heels are the wrong footwear for this. I didn't realize I was taking a trip back in time to the nineteenth century.

Vivian is sitting down on the porch watching her kids run around and occasionally comforting one of them when they fall over. She doesn't stand up when I stagger up to the porch. I sit down without waiting for her to invite me to.

She laughs at me when I groan and pull my shoes off to rub my aching feet. "You can leave them off," she tells me. "Going barefoot is a family tradition around here."

"It isn't very professional, is it? I'm supposed to be interviewing you."

"We can keep it casual. What did you want to ask me about?"

"I'm doing a story on predatory behavior by billionaire men using their money and influence to manipulate and prey on women who are either in subordinate positions or in vulnerable places in their lives. I understand you were working as a secretary before Derek brought you to New York."

"That's true."

"Don't you think it's a little manipulative for a billionaire financial CEO to swoop in and carry off an uneducated secretary?"

She smiles at me. "He wasn't a billionaire financial CEO at the time. He was a penniless salesman who drove a beat-up old car and couldn't even afford to buy himself a decent suit. He was worse off financially than I was—and he didn't carry me off to anywhere. He only got his wealth back after we got involved—and he would have walked away from everything if I had only asked him to. He offered more than once."

I frown at her. "That doesn't seem possible."

"Well, it is. He lost his fortune in a hostile takeover and left New York with nothing. He got a job as a salesman in the company where I worked as an admin clerk. No one knew who he was. I had never even heard of Derek Salazar. We started going out. I didn't find out until later that he was working to build a whole new company in his free time. It took a long time for me to come to terms with even being able to live in New York with him at all. I never wanted the billionaire lifestyle. He offered to move back to New Jersey with me so we could be together even if it meant giving up his new company. I told him he needed to stay because he had contractual obligations and investors who were relying on him. We only stayed together because I found this house. It was the perfect solution and made it comfortable enough for me to stay in New York with him."

"You....*you* were the one who did it?" I shake that out of my head and plow right on with my line of questioning. "But don't you think it's kind of sexist for him to keep you at home to cook and clean instead of letting you pursue your passions? He should want you to succeed if he really loves you."

Now she's the one who blinks at me. Then she looks away. "You're the most badly informed reporter I've ever met."

I wince at those words. *Journalistic integrity.* I don't have nearly as much journalistic integrity as I think I do.

"Why do you say that?" I ask.

"Because Derek does let me pursue my passions. He does a hell of a lot more than let me. He encourages me to. I have my own content creation business with a YouTube channel, paid courses, and consultations. I have over two million subscribers on my channel alone. I could have become a member of The Billionaires' Club if I wanted to, but I decided to scale back my operation so I would have more time to spend with my family."

My eyes pop out of their sockets. "Really? I didn't know that."

"You should. You should have found out everything about me before you contacted me for an interview. Derek was the one who told me I should pursue my passions. He was the one who suggested that I build a business around it so I could share my ideas and passion with the world. I wouldn't have done any of that without his help and guidance."

I don't know what to say. One of her children starts screaming his head off just then and Vivian goes over there to see what the problem is. She picks him up and we see a honeybee buzzing around in the grass. The kid must have stepped on it.

The little boy is blaring so loudly that I can't get a word in. It looks like the interview is over. I yell over the noise to tell Vivian she's given me a lot to think about and to thank her for seeing me.

She smiles, waves at me, and says something, but I can't hear her over the boy's pained bellows.

I have no choice but to put my shoes back on and hike back out to the road. I throw away what little dignity I have left once I get far enough away that Vivian can't see me. I take off my shoes and walk the rest of the way barefoot.

I stand out there on the roadside while I call a cab to come and take me back to Manhattan. I don't know what's going on here. Is it possible that Rory developed some kind of PR campaign to make The Billionaires' Club look better than it is?

I take notes on my phone on the way back to town. I jot down as much as I can remember of what Melody and Vivian told me about their husbands and their involvement in the club. I have some serious research to do when I get home.

The cab pulls up on a tree-lined street in the far northern end of Manhattan. The car stops in front of a huge mansion with a high stone wall surrounding it. Four armed and uniformed security guards stand at the gate.

I pay the cab driver and approach the gate. "My name is Nicole Bates. I'm here to see Jocelyn Hitchcock."

One of the guards makes a phone call. "Yes, Ma'am. There's a Nicole Bates here to see you. Yes, Ma'am. I understand. Thank you."

He hangs up and pushes a button in his gatehouse to open the huge wrought-iron gates. "She says you can go right in. Go up to the front door there. She'll come out and meet you."

I walk up to the mansion's big, imposing front doors. They open from the inside before I get there. A petite Asian woman answers. She's wearing casual jeans, an untucked flannel shirt, and sneakers.

She takes a few sideways lurching steps toward me and I see that her legs are misshapen and bent the wrong way. She has to hobble to move around.

She smiles at me and holds out her hand. "Nicole? I'm Jocelyn. Nice to meet you."

"I....." I look down at her body. "I'm sorry. I don't know what I expected, but this isn't it."

She laughs. "I got shot in the line of duty. I don't work in the field anymore. I have an administrative job with the NYPD now. Come on in. We can go talk in the garden."

She heads back into the house. She walks slowly and her body jerks every time she takes a step. She has to throw her weight to the side and drag her legs forward each time. Walking looks painful for her, but she doesn't complain. She smiles a lot.

I have to walk slowly to keep pace with her. She passes through the enormous mansion to the terrace outside. She lowers herself into a lawn chair under a trellis covered in wisteria. It casts the area in pleasant shade.

I sit down opposite her. I'm just about to launch into my first question, but she cuts me off first. "You might as well know right up front that phone calls about you have been flying back and forth all over town."

I look up. "They are?"

She grins at me. "The people you've already talked to have been calling everyone you haven't talked to and warning us about you."

I look away. "Maybe this was a bad idea."

"It seems like you don't know very much about us. We're a community—a very close-knit community. I didn't think I would ever find a more close-knit and supportive community than the Police Force, but I did."

"You investigated Diego Espinosa for murder and now...." I find myself glancing around at the house. It's magnificent—almost unbelievable in its size, luxury, and appeal.

"Now I'm married to him. You didn't know that, either, did you?"

"But how? How could you marry an accused murderer?"

"The charges were bogus. Someone in the Police Department or maybe in the city hierarchy brought an unfounded accusation against him because he was a member of the club. That's the only reason he was ever arrested. He had an ironclad alibi with hundreds of witnesses confirming that he was nowhere near the location when the victim was killed. Someone in the chain of command got the crazy idea that Diego must be guilty because he was a billionaire—just like you seem to have gotten the idea that all these men must be money-hungry predators because they're billionaires. You need to open your eyes and get the facts. Isn't that what journalistic integrity is?"

There's that word again. Journalistic integrity.

I can't stop now. "How did the investigation unfold?"

"I started to get suspicious when my commanding officer told me to investigate Diego even though all the available evidence indicated that he never should have gotten arrested in the first place. He did CPR to try to save the victim and Diego had no motive to kill him. Then the sergeant in charge of our precinct at the time ordered me and my partner to fabricate evidence implicating Diego. I informed him and his attorney and I lodged a complaint with the Civil Complaints Review Board. My sergeant got fired and the charges against Diego were dropped."

"It's lucky for Diego that he was involved with the detective running the investigation."

"We weren't involved. We didn't get involved until much later." She frowns at me and then looks away shaking her head. "Everything they said about you is true. You really need to do your homework. You should have figured out the timeline between the murder investigation and when Diego and I got involved. It's all public record."

She takes out her phone, unlocks it, and holds it up so I can see the screen. She shows me the article—my article—the one about how there are no good billionaires.

"Have you done any research at all into these men or the companies they run?" she goes on. "I used to be like you. I used to think they were all playing an act and cutting people off at the knees behind the public's back. You should look into all the charitable work these men do, the jobs they've created, and the lives they've changed. Is this really what you wanted when you became a reporter—to go around smearing innocent people who are only trying to do some good in the world?"

I flinch. "No....but I have a job to do...."

"You could be doing your job and maintaining your integrity at the same time. You could be reporting the truth—which is what you're supposed to be doing. You could be making a difference instead of being part of the problem."

She doesn't act like she's in any big hurry to end the interview, but I sure am. How did this happen? I feel like these women are interviewing me instead of the other way around.

I make an excuse to get out of there. Jocelyn starts to stand up, but I insist that I can find my own way out. I have to get away from her. I have to get away from all of them.

What if they're right? What if I'm part of the problem because I'm willing to print any random trash just to get headlines?

Chapter 4: Rory

I leave the buffet to meet up with Kevin Drake to talk to him about the latest PR campaign he wants me to do on People, Inc.'s new youth intervention courses.

I see and hear the same thing everywhere I go in the club. Everyone reads Nicole Bates's latest article about how there's no such thing as a good billionaire.

The news has been flying all over town about her interviews with Jocelyn, Vivian, and Melody. I'm surprised Nicole even published this piece considering what they all told her.

I stop next to a group with Dante, Jackson, Judah, and Giovanni all talking about the same thing.

"Do you really think it was a good idea to take her around the club like that?" Judah asks. "It's bad enough she's writing shit like this about us. You didn't have to give her VIP access to do it."

"Everything in the article is public record," I point out. "She could have found out the truth about Niko and Melody, Vivian and Derek, and Diego and Jocelyn if she'd only looked for it. She probably already knew about it and published this piece anyway. She would have published it whether I let her in or not. At least this way we have a chance to see the attacks coming and counter them if they can be countered at all. Some reporter somewhere is always going to take a shot at us. She isn't unique in that."

"So what are you going to do to control the damage?" Dante asks.

"I say we give her enough rope to hang herself with. She'll either figure it out herself or someone somewhere will fact-check her and realize she pulled it all out of her ass. She'll have no choice but to correct herself and everyone will find out the truth."

"We should publish a rebuttal piece," Camden Klein suggests. "We should publish the facts and point to all the public records proving it."

"The rebuttal can't come from us. That would make us look weak and defensive. We should pretend the piece doesn't bother us and let someone else rebut her instead."

"You're the club's PR officer," Gunner Bonham points out. "Is your strategy really to do nothing? Aren't you going to do anything?"

I try not to sneer at him. He's ten years older than I am, but he's new to the club. "I'm the club's PR officer for a reason. I would do something in a heartbeat if I thought it would actually help. I can promise you I won't do anything if I think it will actively hurt the club. Publishing a piece in our own defense will definitely hurt the club. This Nicole Bates is already out there interviewing people connected to the club. Either she or someone connected with her will figure it out and the whole house of cards will collapse. You'll see."

Kevin gets a phone call just then. He moves the phone away from his mouth. "She's here again," he murmurs. "She's outside causing a disturbance. Let's go."

He and I go downstairs and find all three security guards blockading the entrance while Nicole tries to barge her way in.

"What's the meaning of this, Ms. Bates?" Kevin demands. "I told you before that you wouldn't be allowed to come back inside the club. What part of that did you not understand?"

"You told me I would have to get my information some other way," she fires back. "How am I supposed to do that when everyone in the club keeps stonewalling me?"

"No one is stonewalling you, Ms. Bates," he tells her. "I know for a fact that you've already interviewed three different women who are married to billionaire club members, one of whom is in fact a member of the club and one of the women you say is being so badly mistreated by her husband. You obviously didn't get the answers you wanted from them and you either ignored or deliberately avoided finding out the truth through any honest research into the club. I don't know why you insist on publishing these lies about us, but you won't get any help from us to do it. Now, if you don't leave, we'll have to call the Police." He turns to the security guards. "Give her five minutes to leave. Then call the cops."

He walks back inside. I should do the same thing, but I find myself sticking around to try to reason with her. "Why are you doing this? I stuck my neck out for you last time and this is how you repay me. What the hell are we supposed to think?"

"Just let me back inside one more time. Just let me interview everyone. You wouldn't let me talk to anyone last time..."

"Can you blame me? I would be even more reluctant to let you talk to anyone now. I know for a fact that the women you interviewed defended their husbands and the club—and you went and published this smear piece anyway. What's the matter with you? Don't you have a shred of self-respect?"

"Take me to the next club gala as your date. Then I can interview everyone at the same time. Come on, Rory."

I snort at her. "Uh....no. Just no. I'm not taking you anywhere, especially not on anything you're calling a date. That's the last thing I would do."

"Is that because you're already taking someone? Are you seeing someone? You have no reason not to take me if you aren't taking someone else."

"I'm not seeing anyone and you would be the last person I would ever take to a gala. I would rather hire someone to go as my date than take you. You're actively trying to sabotage the club for no good reason even though you have all the evidence that no one here is doing anything wrong. I won't use my position in the club to help you do it or to help you ambush my friends in a setting that's supposed to be relaxing and friendly."

She hesitates a fraction of a second before she waves it off. "It doesn't matter. I'm sure one of the others will take me. I'm sure there are plenty of younger single men in the club who would want to take me as their date."

I do my best not to roll my eyes at her. "Good luck with that. Now you're just being deliberately annoying to harass us. You won't win any friends that way. Now you better leave." I check my watch. "Your five minutes starts right now."

I give the security guards a look. They've been standing there listening to our conversation, so they heard me say her five minutes started then.

I go back inside and rejoin the group. "You're being way too soft on her, man," Jackson tells me.

"You only say that because you didn't hear the lecture I just gave her outside. Do you want to hear something wild? She actually suggested that I take her to the next gala as my date so she can interview all of you there. She was actually serious."

"She must be really desperate," Judah remarks.

"Desperate to get herself dumped, you mean," Gunner adds.

"I would take her," Camden chimes in. "She's hot. I would take her just for the night. Why not?"

The others groan and throw food at him. "You really must be desperate for a date," Jackson tells him. "Take a real girl who isn't trying to use you for her own gain."

Camden grins at us and pulls out his phone. "Her social media information is at the bottom of the article and so is her email address. I can contact her that way."

Chapter 5: Nicole

I open the door to my apartment and meet up with Camden Klein waiting there to take me to The Billionaires' Club gala.

He's a good-looking guy of about thirty, but he's the most generic kind of good-looking guy I can ever remember meeting. He looks like someone cut him out of a magazine.

I know very little about the guy except that he runs a stock trading business on Wall Street. I'm learning the hard way to research these people before I have anything to do with them.

Camden hasn't done anything to distinguish himself except to make a shitload of money. He had the most mundane middle-class upbringing and his parents loaned him his first stake so he could start trading.

He poses a striking contrast to someone like Rory. They're equally good-looking, but I haven't been able to stop thinking about Rory since I read his story.

He came from nothing. Now he's on top. He's five years younger than Camden, but Rory has a degree of maturity and self-possession I haven't seen in men three times his age. He grew up hard, fast, and he knows the world only too well.

That kind of depth and experience comes out in everything he does. He commands respect. He doesn't expect anyone to respect him because of his money.

Camden reminds me of a little boy in a grown man's body. I would be very surprised if he's ever had to work for anything in his life. He looks like he's had an easy, comfortable existence and he expects to continue to do the same thing.

He bursts into a grin and doesn't even try to stop his eyes from roving down my body to check out my dress. I'm wearing a simple, elegant, cream velvet gown with a low, scoop neckline and simple, tasteful jewelry.

I don't want to overdo it. I don't want to wear anything fake and I can't afford anything fancier than this.

I know I look good in high heels and my hair twisted in an elegant spiral on the back of my head. I finish off my outfit with a gold scarf draped over my arms and behind my back.

His eyes trace all my curves. "Dang," he breathes. "You look delicious."

I try not to make a face. He better not start treating this like a real date. I know Rory told Camden and everyone else at the club about my offer because Camden mentioned it when he contacted me. He said Rory told them I was looking for a date to the gala.

I do my best to smile at Camden, but no force on earth or in heaven can make it a genuine smile. "Shall we go? We don't want to be late."

He offers me his arm and we head down the hall toward the elevator. He leans in close and murmurs, "Maybe we would want to be late."

I keep facing front. "Maybe, but we don't want to be late *now*." I push the button to call the elevator. It takes an age to climb up to my floor.

"You should have come to me first if you wanted to get into the club," he tells me. "I would have gotten you in. You could have been interviewing me all day and all night."

I barely glance at him. I don't tell him he has nothing distinguishing I would want to interview him for.

"Are you predatory on women?" I ask.

He laughs. "Where were you when Giovanni was running wild on the streets? He's the only one who is predatory on women."

I don't look at him at all this time. "Maybe."

We get into the elevator. He keeps trying to talk to me on the way downstairs. "How did you get into journalism?" he asks.

"I ran my high school newspaper and studied journalism in college."

"Are you one of the founders of the *New York Record*? Is it a passion project for you? Is that why you haven't applied to one of the bigger papers?"

I choose to ignore the obvious veiled insult implying I couldn't get a job at a bigger paper. I just say, "No, I'm not one of the founders."

We get to the bottom of the elevator shaft just then. He leads the way through the building lobby. A long, sleek black limo is waiting for us at the curb.

I start to get a very bad feeling about this when I realize I'll be riding in the back of the car alone with him. I should have thought this through more carefully. Now I can't get out of it.

We get into the car. Camden sits way too close to me and keeps trying to make suggestions that we might actually be interested in each other. He can't possibly think that—not about me, at least.

Maybe he thinks I'll fall for him because he's a billionaire and a member of the club. I would never go out with a guy like him.

It isn't that he isn't attractive because he is. He's drop-dead hot. He's just extremely shallow. There's no substance behind the curtain. He's completely two-dimensional. He talks the whole way to the gala without ever scratching the surface.

He asks a lot of questions about me, what I do, how I started working for the *Record*—all of that. We would probably have a good conversation if this was any other date.

He already knows it isn't. He knows I'm doing this to interview the club members. So why is he trying to show interest in me?

I put up with it for the ride there. I might have to shut him down if he thinks he's going to hook up with me afterward as some kind of payment for taking me.

He offers me his arm again on the way into the Four Seasons Hotel. He fills the airwaves the whole time telling me about how the club used to change the gala venue every time, but now they hold it at the same place four times a year—like I care about that.

He doesn't notice my silence—or maybe he just likes the sound of his own voice. We walk into the grand ballroom and I immediately start spotting the people I want to interview.

Rory stands on the opposite side of the room talking to four other men—Jackson Metcalf, Dante Helme, Gunner Bonham, and Zane Vancroft.

Rory looks outstanding in a spotless black tux. They all look outstanding, but he especially stands out to me. I don't know why. Maybe it's because he's the one who has been the most willing to talk to me.

He makes a brief moment of eye contact with me when I walk in. Then he goes back to talking to his friends. Did he tell everyone that I would be here and why? I would expect nothing less from him.

Camden takes me around introducing me to everyone. The billionaires and their wives are perfectly polite, welcoming, and friendly toward me.

Niko is here, but Melody isn't. I'm not surprised and no one else acts like him being here alone is anything to worry about. Jocelyn is here, but Vivian isn't. Jocelyn smiles at me and tells me it's nice to see me again. She actually acts like she means it.

I don't see anyone giving me dirty looks. Maybe they don't mind that Camden brought me as his date.

Chapter 6: Nicole

C amden gets me a glass of champagne from the gala wet bar, goes off somewhere to talk to some people, and I make a beeline for a group of women standing to one side of the buffet. Mckenna Pearson Metcalf, Emberlynn Rhinehart, and Piper Legrange stand together talking.

"Alvin would love it if you came over again," Mckenna is saying when I pull up. "He had a great time last time we saw each other."

"That would be great." Emberlynn turns to me and holds out her hand. "You must be Nicole. We've heard a lot about you."

I try not to make a face. "I'm sure none of it was good."

She smiles at me. "I'm actually really glad you're here. We can talk here and get it out of the way. Then you don't have to track me down and maybe catch me at a less convenient time."

"Is it inconvenient for you to give interviews when MegaDome is coming up?" I ask.

"It isn't that. I'm just so busy with the boys and everything—and the house is never clean when you have two kids running around. I would be embarrassed for you to come over then."

"Try it with four and see how you like it," Mckenna interjects.

I raise my eyebrows at Emberlynn. "I didn't realize that you and Dante had kids."

"We adopted them. Their parents died in a car accident and we took the boys when they were four and two so they wouldn't go into the foster system. We have a permanent placement now so we're raising them as our own. Neither of them remembers the accident or anything about their lives before their parents died. We're the only parents they've ever known."

"But....isn't Dante.....isn't he like.....old enough to be their grand-father?"

She bursts out laughing. "Yeah! He has grandkids who are older than our boys. Can you believe that?!" She laughs some more, elbows Mckenna, and they share a knowing look. "Alvin is so great with them. I'm really glad they have him as a big brother to look up to."

"What about Jay and Lucas?" Piper adds. "They're your boys' big brothers, too."

"And don't forget Todd," Mckenna chimes in.

All three of them explode with laughter like that's the funniest thing ever. I don't know the people they're talking about, so I don't get the joke.

I try to steer this train back onto the rails. I'm supposed to be conducting a professional interview here. "Is it true that Dante was mentoring you in business when you started MegaDome? Did he give you the idea?"

Emberlynn gets serious all of a sudden. "He did give me the idea, but not in the way you think. He didn't come out and say, 'You will start the MegaDome Experience, young padawan'." She uses a deep, chesty, commanding tone and points at me when she says it.

Piper and Mckenna fall over each other laughing again.

"How did he give you the idea, then?" I ask.

"He started telling me about how I should think of any job I took as working for myself even if someone else paid my paycheck. He said I should take ownership of the job, myself, and my future instead of just floating along as a mindless worker drone—which is what I was doing. I did some project management in a previous position, so the idea of working for myself came out of that. That's what gave me the idea. He didn't know anything about it until after I came up with the idea. I had already booked Madison Square Garden for the first MegaDome by the time he found out about that."

"And were you involved with each other then?"

"Not in any kind of serious way. We hooked up once before that—very casually—a long time before that. It was a totally meaningless one-night thing. We never saw each other again after that."

"So.....would you say he hooked up with you to take advantage of you?"

She laughs in my face. "Definitely not. It was definitely mutual and he definitely did not take advantage of me."

"But you knew he was a billionaire, didn't you. Did you hook up with him because of that?"

"That isn't why I did it. I did it because he was one of the nicest guys I had ever met. He was really nice to me and helped me when I needed it. He treated me better than any other guy I had ever gone out with—and then he did the same thing *after* we got together. He was always there for me and we helped each other through some very dark times. I wouldn't want to go through that with anyone else—and I wouldn't want to have kids with anyone else, either."

"Did getting together with him mean you couldn't have kids of your own? Is that why you adopted instead of having your own—because he was too old?"

She beams at me. "No. That wasn't the reason at all. He got himself tested and he could still have kids of his own. He was perfectly healthy. I didn't have to give up anything to get with him—and adopting the boys with him has been the best thing that has ever happened to me. I have the life of my dreams thanks to him."

I glance back and forth between Piper and Mckenna. "What about you?" I ask Mckenna. "I know you worked as Jackson's assistant for years. Did he use his position to maneuver you into a relationship with him?"

She clucks her tongue and shakes her head. "You really don't know what you're talking about, do you? Vivian and Melody said it was true, but I didn't think it was this bad."

"Why? What do you mean? That's what I'm here for—to find out the truth."

"You would already know that if you just got on the computer and did your job. I quit working as Jackson's assistant when I got a terminal cancer diagnosis. The doctors only gave me a few months to live and I was raising two kids alone. I thought we would have to move into a homeless shelter and my kids would go into foster care after I was gone, but Jackson stepped in and took all of us in. He gave us a house of our own and set up trust funds to send my kids to boarding school after I was gone. He got attached to them and offered to give them a home and raise them after I was gone. He did all of that long before there was ever anything going on between us. He never wanted anything from me except to help out my family and make sure my kids were taken care of. That's the kind of man he is. He just wanted to make sure my kids got the life they deserved after I wasn't around to give it to them myself. He couldn't stand to watch my kids go into foster care when he had the power to stop it."

Her story strikes a white-hot bolt of lightning through me—and I realize. She's right. I would know all of this if I had only researched these people beforehand. I would have been able to see that she stopped working for Jackson before they got involved.

What was I thinking? I already know the answer to that. I thought I knew all I needed to know before I started doing the story. I had already made up my mind about these people long before I ever met them.

I do my best not to show how much her story affects me. "So how did you get involved? You obviously didn't die. What happened?"

"We got involved after I started getting sick. The cancer progressed much faster than any of us realized. I was already weak and getting weaker and sicker by the day by the time we got together. He just wanted to be there and love me and the kids as much as possible in the time we had left. He wanted to make sure I had everything I needed and that I didn't have to worry about the kids so I could die peacefully and without any stress. He wanted to bond with the kids so he could be there for them the way they would need him to after they lost me. We became a family. It happened really fast and my kids gravitated to him. He moved into their lives and started being the father they needed him to be. He was there for them when I went into the hospital and they all thought I was going to die."

"How did you beat it?"

She bursts into a huge smile. "I got pregnant. I got pregnant from Jackson and the hormones sent me into remission. We still didn't know how long I would have, but the pregnancy reversed it and I started to recover. Now my kids consider Jackson their dad and we have two kids of our own." She blushes and looks down at the floor with tears in her eyes. "He's an angel. He's my angel. He's like some kind of saint or something."

"He certainly is," Piper murmurs and Emberlynn squeezes Mckenna's arm.

I stare at all three of them. This is beyond anything I ever expected to hear. That word blasts my world apart. Angel. She considers her former boss an angel.

My eyes dart across the room to Jackson. He doesn't look like an angel. He looks like a machine. He looks like someone I wouldn't want to meet in a dark alley in the middle of the night—or anywhere else for that matter. He looks downright dangerous.

There must be another side to him if he could do something like this. Maybe my impressions of all of these people are wrong.

Isn't that what I keep hearing from everyone—that the members of The Billionaires' Club are really just good people trying to do some good in the world? Why do I find that so hard to believe?

Who would know that better than their wives? I glance in the other direction. Niko is talking to Kevin Drake and Paige Novak across the ballroom. She stands with her arm around Kevin's waist and his arm around her shoulders.

She turns her head in the middle of their conversation and kisses him on the cheek. It's such an intimate act. None of these women act like beaten down, manipulated, preyed-on victims of anything or anyone.

Paige Novak is a billionaire in her own right. She's a titan of the industry and everyone respects her. She stands over there oozing confidence, grace, and feminine allure. She engages Niko in conversation as much as Kevin does.

I see the same thing everywhere I look. Everything I knew about these people is wrong. Maybe there are some good billionaires after all. In fact, I'm in a room full of them right this very minute.

I need to get out of here and think about this. I down the rest of my champagne, set the glass on the nearest server's tray, and cross the room to intercept Camden.

I plan to excuse myself, tell him I'm not feeling too good, and catch a cab home. I don't want to wait around for him to try to make a move on me.

I make it halfway across the ballroom and stop in my tracks. I look around everywhere and see Rory watching me again. He's the only person in the room who even seems to be aware of me.

Something is wrong. I don't know what it is, but I really don't feel good all of a sudden. I'm not faking and I won't be making an excuse. I feel lightheaded and sick to my stomach all of a sudden.

Rory's gaze becomes oppressive. I can't let him see me like this. I don't want him to find out what I just learned about Jackson and Mckenna.

Rory must already know about that. They all know. Everyone here already knows what I just found out. I'm the last to wake up from the illusion.

I head off in another direction looking for the bathroom. I don't want to puke in the middle of the ballroom.

Chapter 7: Rory

I study Nicole while she interviews Emberlynn Rhinehart and Mckenna Pearson Metcalf. I can only imagine what they're telling her about how predatory, manipulative, and misogynistic Jackson and Dante are.

What a joke that is. I can't think of any kinder, nicer, more considerate men anywhere. I wish I could be as good as they are. Maybe someday I'll grow up enough to be like them.

I hope she's finally getting the message. I don't know how many other women she has to interview before she gets it through her head.

She tosses her drink, puts her glass down, and heads across the ballroom to meet back up with Camden.

He better be treating her right and he better not have brought her to the gala thinking he could get something out of her in exchange. He better not be trying to use her. She might be a reporter. She might even be a dirtbag reporter. She doesn't deserve that.

She stops in the middle of the ballroom, looks around, and spots me. She stares at me for a long time. I can't read her expression. I should probably intervene to get her out of here before she does any more damage to the club.

I did all I could by warning everyone about her beforehand. Everyone here knows why she's here and why she's asking these questions.

Everyone here already knows about her article and the interviews she's done with Melody, Vivian, and Jocelyn.

I don't know what else I can do besides stand back and watch it all burn to the ground. She's going to have a rude awakening when it does happen.

She stares at me for way too long. Why? Then I see her swaying. Does she even realize something is wrong with her?

I make the decision to put my drink down, go over there, and find a way to escort her out of the ballroom as politely and discreetly as possible. This whole catastrophe has gone on long enough.

She breaks away before I can move, staggers back the way she came, and rushes off toward the bathroom. I leave it alone. I don't want to get involved in that.

Camden is too busy talking to other people and laughing at their jokes. He stands with his back to the room. He didn't even keep an eye on her. What a troll. No wonder he's still single.

I observe the rest of the gala while I wait for Nicole to come out. I'll escort her out as soon as she finishes in the bathroom. Then everyone else will be able to relax and enjoy themselves without her around.

She doesn't come out for a long time—too long. I glance in that direction, but I don't see her coming out of the bathroom. Maybe something really is wrong.

That's the moment when I see one of the servers standing down there. He's a young guy wearing the same black tux as all the other male servers. He would look exactly the same as the club members, but he isn't a club member.

He stands at the entrance to the women's bathroom—the same bathroom where I've been watching and waiting for Nicole to come out. That on its own raises my suspicions.

The guy pushes the door open an inch, peeks in, and then glances left and right to make sure no one is watching him. He doesn't see me across the ballroom. Then he pushes the door all the way open and ducks inside.

I don't waste time explaining what I'm doing to Dante and Jackson. I storm across the ballroom. That cocksucker better not be planning what I think he's planning.

The bathroom door is shut again by the time I get there. I don't bother to check and see if any women are in the bathroom. He's in there. That's all I need to know.

I walk in, and yes, he is doing what I thought he was planning to do. He lies on the floor in an open stall with Nicole lying flat on her stomach underneath him. She's obviously out cold with both arms lying limp at her sides.

He's hiked her dress up to her waist. He crams his hips between her bare legs from behind while he tries to scoot down her panties with one hand and his own pants with the other. I can't believe what I'm seeing.

I don't hesitate an instant. I storm in, grab the guy by the collar, and vent all my fury on him by yanking him off her. She doesn't move. She lies there completely unconscious.

I rip him out of the stall and slam him face down on the floor. I don't even try to be gentle, the cocksucking piece of shit!

He bellows out in pain and surprise. "Shut the fuck up, you son of a bitch!" I roar. "Get down before I send you to the fucking hospital!"

I lift him a little bit and slam him down a second time just for good measure. He tries to struggle, but I'm not in any mood to take it easy on the guy. I pin my knee against the back of his neck and my other leg across his hips to hold him down.

I yank my phone out of my pocket and call 911. I'm breathing too hard. I have to fight my voice under control so I can talk to the dispatcher.

The dispatcher is a man with a deep, gruff voice. "911 emergency dispatch. Please state the nature of the emergency."

"I just caught some guy....trying to assault a woman....in the women's bathroom.....at the Four Seasons Hotel.....I'm restraining him.....she looks.....she's unconscious.....she might be.....I don't k now......"

His tone changes instantly. "You said you're at the Four Seasons Hotel? Is that correct?"

"Yeah!" I pant. "In the ballroom......at the......The Billionaires' Club gala.....he's one of the servers.....the woman.....she's a guest....."

"I'm dispatching Police and an ambulance now, Sir. Is the woman stable?"

"I......" I don't know what to do, but fortunately for me, Jackson pushes the door open a crack at that moment. I wave him inside and move the phone away from my mouth. "Hold the bastard down. Don't let him move."

Jackson comes over and plants his foot on the back of the assailant's neck. I hustle over to the stall and quickly pull Nicole's dress down before I do anything else.

I squat down to check her pulse. "She still has a pulse," I tell the dispatcher. "And she's breathing."

"Can you assess her level of consciousness? Is she completely unconscious or just partially? Is she under the influence of any substance?"

"Um....."

I don't know what to do or say, so I put the phone down for a second, gather Nicole in my arms as well as I can in this cramped stall, and pull her out onto the floor next to the server.

I roll her onto her back. Her eyes are partially open. "Nicole?" I ask. "Can you hear me? The ambulance is on the way. Just hold on a little longer. The Police and ambulance are coming to take you to the hospital."

I don't get any response, so I pick up the phone. "I can't tell if she can hear me or not. She isn't moving at all, but her eyes are partway open."

"Stay with her, Sir, and continue to monitor her pulse and respirations until emergency services get there."

"Yeah...." I gasp. "I am. My friend is here to help me control the attacker."

"Thank you, Sir. Police are at the building entrance. They should be with you shortly."

I catch Jackson giving me a strange look. I check on Nicole again and make sure she's presentable enough for the medics to take her out of here with her dignity intact.

The Police storm the bathroom first. They cuff the attacker and the paramedics move in to load Nicole onto their gurney. The cops take me and Jackson off to one side to ask what happened.

I give a statement about what I found the attacker doing in the bathroom. The rest of the guests and gala attendees stand around whispering to each other while the paramedics wheel Nicole out into the night.

Chapter 8: Nicole

I groan when I open my eyes. Harsh white fluorescent light stabs me in the brain and I raise my hand to cover my eyes.

That one moment gives me one brief glimpse of Rory Kahn sitting in a chair by my bed. He's still wearing the tux he had on at the gala. He watches me with his usual hawkish expression.

"Oh, my God!" I moan. "I don't believe it!"

"How are you feeling?" he asks. "The doctors say you'll probably be a little lightheaded and unsteady for a few days."

I try to look around and wind up squinting again. "I'm in the hospital!" I croak. "Oh, my God! This is the worst night of my life."

"One of the servers spiked your drink," he tells me. "Don't worry. The guy is under arrest for attacking you."

I can't look at him. I keep my hand over my eyes. "I remember. I remember everything, Rory. I remember you coming into the bathroom and I remember you trying to talk to me."

He doesn't answer. He's sitting there next to my hospital bed. He's the one who saved me from that guy trying to attack me when I was drugged and defenseless on the bathroom floor.

That would have been my worst nightmare—to have to lie there feeling, hearing, and remembering everything while he did that.

I would have been fully awake and aware of everything—every sensation—every feral grunt of satisfaction as he attacked my helpless body.....

I can't even look at Rory. I don't even care that he saw me half-naked with my dress pushed up over my bare ass and that he saw some guy trying to pull my panties down.

He saved me. Rory saved me. He's one of them. He's one of the men in the club who is just trying to help people. He's been trying to help me since I first showed up at the club.

I can't even summon the courage to thank him—or to apologize for making such a mess of things.

We're still sitting here in silence—or I'm lying here in silence. Some of the nurses come in to check on me. I have an IV hooked up to my arm. They take my vital signs and shine a light in my eyes. Then they talk to Rory about discharging me.

"She shouldn't drive or operate machinery for twenty-four hours until her system has a chance to metabolize more of the drugs out of her bloodstream," one of the nurses tells him.

"Don't worry," he replies. "I'll drive her home."

Of course. He's sitting here taking care of me even now—even after what I did to the club.

Journalistic integrity. I must not have any journalistic integrity at all. That's what he said. I would have checked my facts before I published that article if I had any integrity as a journalist. I would have made sure whatever I was printing was factually accurate.

The nurses leave and come back with my discharge paperwork. I have to squint to focus my eyes well enough to scrawl my name at the bottom of the documents. I still feel half-drunk on the drugs.

The nurses leave me alone with Rory. He would sit there in silence just watching over me. He wouldn't say a word about what I did to the club or how badly I botched this whole thing.

"Thank you," I finally croak. "For everything.....and I'm sorry.....I know I messed up...."

"I really wish I could believe you," he murmurs back. "You either knew about all of this or you were too blasé about your job to care. I can't overlook that. None of us can. You could have ruined everything for us—for nothing. You had no reason whatsoever to try to make us look bad. You did it for no reason at all. You even found out what was going on and you still didn't print any retraction or correction of your original article. What are we supposed to think? Now your work is out there tarnishing the reputations of good people who do a lot of good for a lot of people. You did that. It's going to take a lot more than saying you're sorry and thanking me to correct that. I hope you realize t hat now."

"I do...... I just....."

A uniformed Police officer comes into the room just then. He's a middle-aged guy with a double chin. "I found out what you wanted to know, Mr. Kahn," he tells Rory.

Rory stands up to meet him. "What's the story? The guy worked for the catering service. He wasn't connected to the club."

"Yes, Sir. That's what we found out. The booking officer ran his prints and a DNA sample through the database as soon as the officers got the suspect down to the precinct. He's wanted for five other drug-related assaults. He's already gone up for bail and been denied." The officer glances at me. "He won't be getting out before his plea hearing."

"Thank you, Officer." Rory sticks out his hand. "That's a relief. I really appreciate you coming to tell us."

The officer shakes hands and leaves us alone. Rory sits back down in his chair. He doesn't say another word to me. He's already said enough—and he's right about all of it.

I'm the one who screwed this up. I screwed it up by being a shitty reporter and a shitty human being.

Everyone at the club has been polite, forthcoming, and welcoming to me. None of them has pushed me away for being a shitty reporter and a shitty human being even though I'm both.

Now he's here taking care of me. He saved me from that guy. Rory called 911 for me and now he's been sitting here next to my bed the whole time. He'll drive me home after this so I don't have to worry about how I'm going to get there.

He would probably go a lot further than that. He would have gone a lot further to stop that guy from hurting me. Rory does all of this because he's a good person. He does the right thing. He isn't a shitty human being—not the way I painted all of them at the club.

I called him a spin doctor, but he isn't one. He's just a decent guy—a lot more decent than some.

The nurses come back to tell me I can leave the hospital. It takes me a long time to get up. I have to sit on the edge of the bed for a while before my head stops swimming.

Rory comes over to me and puts a brown leather bomber jacket around my shoulders. Don't ask me where he got it. It's probably his. He uses it to cover me up so I'm not walking around the hospital in the middle of the night in a strapless evening gown.

My voice cracks when I thank him again. He's one of the most attentive and considerate men I've ever met.

He does everything without a hint of subtext. He isn't doing this to imply anything or to start anything. He does it to be attentive and considerate—because I'm vulnerable and fragile right now.

He doesn't respond when I thank him. He'll go through this whole thing without saying another word to me. We aren't friends—not after the way I acted.

He stands near me keeping an eye on me. He doesn't move to intervene when I finally haul myself to my feet and steady myself against the bed. I'm finally ready to walk out of the room.

He will step in if I need him to. That's what he's here for—to make sure I'm all right. Is he doing this for the club—to make sure the club is protected from any accusation that they caused all of this—or that they allowed it to happen by not being vigilant enough?

He was vigilant enough. He was the one who stopped it from happening. It would have happened right there in the women's bathroom if he hadn't done something.

He and everyone else in the club probably thinks I will accuse them. They probably think I'll hold them responsible and maybe sue for millions of dollars. Why shouldn't they expect that after the way I acted?

I really need to change everything about the way I do this job. It's unacceptable. I'm unacceptable. I can't be this person.

I blunder out of the hospital. He stays by my side the whole way just to make sure I make it all right.

I don't know where to go. He doesn't move or speak until we get to the lobby entrance doors. Then he just says, "This way," and leads me to one side.

He escorts me into the parking lot, between the parked cars, and stops me next to a glossy black BMW coupe. He opens the door for me to get into the passenger seat. Is this his car? I thought he would be driving around in a limo.

He starts the motor and cruises out onto the street. He doesn't say a word until he drives all the way back to my building. It's the middle of the night, so he doesn't have any trouble finding a parking space right in front of the door.

He lets me out of the passenger door again. I can't even look at him. I'm taking the walk of shame. At least he's the one here to see me like this. At least he's the only one.

I can trust him not to think the worst of me. He knows I screwed up. He knows I'm a shitty reporter and a shitty human being, but he takes care of me anyway. He guards me from anything bad happening to me. He doesn't rub it in.

We get into the elevator. He stays with me all the way to the door of my apartment.

I turn around and finally, finally summon the courage to look him in the eye. I feel beaten and bruised. I don't even care that he's seeing me at my lowest.

It makes me feel better in a way that the one person seeing me like this is the one person I most trust to see me like this. I'm sure he's been worse. He doesn't think less of me for it.

It's somehow comforting to know that he couldn't possibly think less of me and yet he still treats me with respect. He treats me with the respect due another human being, even a shitty human being.

"Thank you, Rory," I mumble. "I won't forget this."

"Do you want me to stick around for a while? I will if you don't want to stay alone."

"You don't have to." My throat hurts. "Thank you for offering. I'll be all right now."

"I'm sorry this happened at the club. It shouldn't have. I'm sorry it happened at all. No one deserves that."

I can't hold his eye. "Don't apologize. Please."

"Are you gonna be okay? Here. Take this." He hands me a business card with a phone number scrawled on the back in handwritten ballpoint pen. "That's my number. I want you to call me if you need anything. Okay?"

I look down at the number. He's not trying to give me a hint about anything. He's worried about me.

I make the decision then and there not to call him—ever. That's the best way I can repay his help and kindness. I have to disappear out of his life forever.

I've been nothing but a burden and a nightmare to everyone in the club. They've been kind, welcoming, and helpful to me and I've treated them the opposite.

I have to vanish out of their lives like I never existed. That's the best and only way I can correct the mistakes I made.

"Go on inside," he murmurs. "I won't feel right until I see that you're safe."

I tug off the jacket and hand it back to him. "Thank you for letting me use this. I really appreciate it.'

"Keep it," he tells me. "I don't need it."

"No, really. You've done enough. I couldn't take anything else from you."

He takes the jacket out of my hands. His eyes overflow with concern and some deeper kind of understanding.

This man standing in front of me—he's lived through the worst any human can live through. That's what makes him so compassionate and attentive. He's acutely tuned to any human suffering no matter what it is.

I'll never forget him bending over me and trying to make me hear him. *Nicole? Can you hear me?*

He cares—about everyone. That's the truth. He cares that I'm hurting right now and that I could have gotten a lot more hurt if not for his intervention.

I can't stand the look in his eyes. I don't know if I can cope with anyone caring about me that much. He's a total stranger and maybe even my enemy, but he cares more than anyone I've ever met.

He would do a lot more to help me. He would do anything I needed if he thought for an instant that he could help me. That's the kind of man I'm dealing with here.

His attitude reminds me of Mckenna's story about Jackson. *He's an angel. He's my angel. He's like some kind of saint or something.*

That's Rory. He's a genuinely good person who can't stand to see another person suffer.

I know what I have to do. I mumble, "Good night, Rory. Thank you for everything. I'm forever in your debt," and unlock my door.

He says, "Good night," and the door shuts between us. I stumble to the couch and slump on it. He isn't here anymore—and yet he is. I still have his card with his number on it.

I could call on him for help again if I needed it, but I won't. I don't want to make myself a burden to him anymore—or to anyone else in the club.

I should go to bed—and I do. I go into my room, change out of my dress, put on my pajamas, and crawl into bed.

I take my laptop with me and start writing another story—the story I should have written the first time.

I write all the stories I've heard from all the people I've interviewed. I stay up almost all night researching all their claims. Each of them was telling the truth. The information is right there in the public record for anyone to see.

I include the story about Lane Prince going to prison for two years for beating up the guy who tried to prostitute Lane's younger sister. I include the story about Judah Hayes saving Piper Legrange from his deranged, violent ex-wife.

I include the story about Niko Holloway saving Melody from her deranged, violent brother after he kidnapped her and held her as a prisoner. I include the story about the car crash that killed Dante's and Emberlynn's foster sons' parents.

I include the story about Jackson taking in Mckenna and her children, becoming her children's legal guardian, and then marrying Mckenna when she went into remission.

I include the story about certain members of the Police Department manipulating the evidence to frame Diego Espinosa for a murder he didn't commit. I include Jocelyn's complaint report exposing the plot and exonerating Diego of suspicion.

I find a lot more stories I should have found before I published the first article. I include a vast list of examples of charitable activity by everyone in the club. I include some personal interest pieces where certain billionaires have helped their employees and random civilians off the record.

I retract everything and finish the story by saying I'm ashamed of my total lack of journalistic integrity. I published unsubstantiated accusations when all of this information was freely available on the internet.

I take full responsibility and admit plainly that I should have found all of this information before I ever tried to speak to anyone from the club. I take full responsibility for publishing the article before I checked my facts.

I include a laundry list of citations so anyone can go back and check the facts for themselves. I invite the reader to do so as well before anyone passes judgment on these people simply because they have a higher net worth than the rest of us.

I reread the article just as the sun is coming up. I attach the finished article in an email to my editor, but I also send the article to five other outlets I know will publish it. The information needs to be out there.

I did this. I made this mess. Now it's my job to clean it up. I won't shirk that responsibility this time.

I hit *Send* and close my computer. It's done. Now I can start to rebuild from the ground up to become the journalist I'm supposed to be—the journalist I should have been in the first place.

Chapter 9: Nicole

I come out of the *New York Record* office building and turn right on my way down the street. I have to meet up with someone to do an interview for my latest story.

A guy hustles up next to me on the sidewalk. "Nicole Bates?" he asks.

I glance over at a young guy with short brown hair, brown eyes, glasses, and a neat, business-casual outfit. "Yeah?" I ask.

"I'm Scott Presley. Can I talk to you for a second?"

I don't stop walking. "You'll have to make it quick. I have to be somewhere."

"I'm a reporter with the *Atlantic Connection*. I'm doing a story on The Billionaires' Club. I read your previous work that you did with them nine months ago. I wondered if you could take some time to answer a few questions about how you got access to them and how you got so much information about their activities."

"I thought I was pretty clear on that in my second article," I reply over my shoulder. "I found all of that information on the internet....and you'll do the same thing if you have a shred of journalistic integrity."

He actually laughs at that. Great. Now I know everything I need to know about this guy.

"How did you get so many interviews with the club members and their wives?" he asks.

"It wasn't that difficult. All you have to do is call them up. They're perfectly willing to give interviews to anyone who asks. Just make sure you interview them and get all the information before you write your story."

"Are you sure that's all you did? You made it sound like you had close, intimate contact with them."

I snort under my breath. This dude doesn't have a flipping clue—about anything. "I didn't have any close intimate contact with them that anyone else couldn't have. I did nothing special, believe me—and all the information I got is freely available on the internet."

"I've seen all of that. I want more."

I stop in my tracks. I have to think about it before I make the decision to turn around and face the guy. "You've seen it all. You've read all the citations I mentioned in my second article."

"Yep." He nods. "Every last one of them."

"So what is it you want? What more is there?"

"Well, there must be something. This is just what's available to the public. It's what the club members want the public to see. They obviously don't reveal anything going on behind the scenes. They're billionaires. Why do you think they keep so much security around them?"

"Maybe because they don't want random lunatics deciding to come around and break into their houses and bump one of them off just because the club members happen to have money. Maybe they don't want some random stranger to decide they have the right to just barge in and demand answers about the club members' private lives. These people do have a right to privacy, you know. They have that right as much as you or I do. If the club members keep their private lives behind closed doors, then that's nothing more or less than any law-abiding citizen deserves, is it?"

I turn away and keep walking. He shadows me for a while. "What did they say to convince you that they're all so good and upright? You started off investigating them. You could have uncovered more, but you bought their PR narrative hook, line, and sinker. What did they do? Did they pay you off or something?"

"You look into the club all you want, Mr. Presley," I reply over my shoulder. "I'm sure you'll find out what the club and its members are really all about. Have a nice day."

He finally drops off and leaves me alone. I'm quite certain he'll find out what the club and its members are all about. Anyone who looks into the club will find out the same thing. There is only one thing there for anyone to find out—the truth.

I finish my interview and go on about my day. I don't hear anything else about it until a week later.

I'm just writing up my latest story and getting it ready to turn in when one of my colleagues comes up to me at my desk. "Did you see the latest *Connection* story on The Billionaires' Club? The writer mentioned you."

I didn't see the story before now. I shouldn't look at it. The club doesn't concern me. I haven't seen or heard from anyone in the club for more than nine months.

My curiosity gets the better of me and I navigate to the *Atlantic Connection's* website. The Scott Presley piece is right there on the front page.

He's investigating, all right, but most of his article includes all the same unfounded conjecture and innuendo I used in my first piece. He references my citations, but he continues to imply that this is some kind of PR stunt the club is using to hide its true nature.

He finishes the article by quoting what I told him on the street. He makes the same suggestion that I got too close to the truth and the club either paid me off or dug up some kind of dirt on me and blackmailed me to back off and paint them as good and noble.

I click away from the story in disgust. I knew I shouldn't have read it. Now I need to take a long, hot shower.

I have my own business to attend to, so I pretend the *Connection* story never happened. The Billionaires' Club and everything related to it aren't my problem to solve.

I succeed in forgetting about it until another two weeks pass. One of my fellow reporters at the *Record* has a birthday and we all go out to the Castle Brewery for dinner and drinks after work.

We're all standing and sitting around at multiple tables talking about anything and everything. I'm trying to dodge Payton Rogers and Jyro Evenbeck, both of whom are trying to hit on me—occasionally at the same time.

I burst out of a cluster where they're both standing way too close. I grab my empty glass and make an excuse to go to the bar for a refill. I take my friend Maisey's glass with me so the guys understand that I legit had to go to the bar right then.

I put the glasses on the bar, tell the bartender what I want, and wait for him to fill my order. He's really busy right then with multiple waiters coming to the bar with more orders plus all the other customers standing around waiting.

"Nicole?" another man asks from the stool on my left. "Nicole Bates?"

I turn around and come face to face with Rory Kahn. He's sitting on the barstool next to me.

"Hey!" I greet him. "How are you doing? You look great."

He smiles at me. "So do you. How have you been? I haven't seen you in ages."

"I know! I've been keeping my head down and my nose to the grindstone—you know! Just working a lot and trying to stay out of trouble. How about you? How's the PR business?"

He grins even more broadly. "It's very good. Everything is good. Not much has changed since I saw you last. Thank you, by the way. Thank you for sticking up for the club in that *Connection* piece. I really appreciate it."

I roll my eyes and turn back to the bar. "It was the least I could do after the way I acted before. I tried to clean up the mess I made of all of your lives. I wish I could have done more, but I figured the best I could do was to quietly back away and vanish into the wallpaper."

His eyes twinkle. "Thank you. You definitely made up for it with your second story. We're all grateful. *I'm* grateful."

"Please. Don't start being grateful to me. I couldn't stand that. Anyway, it didn't do much good, did it? Presley still published all that venom about you and then he had the nerve to suggest that you blackmailed me or something. You just can't win, can you?"

He won't stop smiling at me. "I'm glad someone out there understands."

"I told him to go ahead and look all he wants. He won't find anything except more of what I found. Then he'll have mud on his face and have to do the walk of shame. Some people just never learn, you know? I'm starting to wonder if he even read my citations."

"Do you think so? He sounded pretty certain about it from what I read."

"That's the problem. He said it was all a PR campaign." I wince. "I shouldn't be talking to you about this."

"It's okay. I'm glad we could finally clear the air—and I'm glad I don't have to continue to think the worst of you."

I grimace. "I wouldn't blame you if you did. You were dead right about me not having any journalistic integrity. That's been my focus these last nine months—trying to get back some of the self-respect I lost during the investigation. I've been trying to rebuild my reputation with myself, you know? Trying to be the journalist I wanted to be when I started. Talking to you made me realize I wasn't—and not just that I wasn't, but how far I really had gone astray from my own standards. It was embarrassing." I wave that away. "Anyway, I don't want to talk about it anymore. I'm just trying to do better now."

"You are doing better. You stuck your neck out for us and we appreciate it. *I* appreciate it. It makes me believe you really have changed."

"I hope so." I turn to him. "How about you? I can't believe nothing has changed for you in nine months."

He shrugs, but his eyes keep twinkling. He looks genuinely happy to see me—which is a nice change. "You know me. Business changes. My life doesn't really change."

"Why not? Does it really make you so happy to be such a monk? You don't have to keep locking yourself away because of...."

I trail off. I don't want to say he's doing it because of his history. I don't really know that much about him. Maybe that isn't the reason he always lives alone.

He reads my thoughts and doesn't answer—at least, he doesn't answer that. He faces front and takes a sip of his drink. He's drinking a pint of beer. It looks like one of the Castle Brewery's house reds.

"Anyway, running PR for the club is a full-time job," he goes on. "Someone is always out to paint us as devils from Hell. I'll never understand why everyone hates the club so much. It isn't like there aren't other billionaires in the world. It seems like people hate us especially for having a club of our own. It's fine for everyone else who wants to talk about their model trains and their chamber music and what books they're reading—but not for us. The world can tolerate us as long as we don't congregate in one place."

I stare at him as a bunch of puzzle pieces click into place in my brain. Not everyone hates The Billionaires' Club—just certain people.

He cocks his head to frown at me. "Are you okay?"

"Yes!" I snap out of it, shake the fog out of my brain, and impulsively squeeze his arm. "It was really great to see you. I'll catch you later. Have a good one."

"Okay. See you later."

I spin away. I don't even stick around long enough to get my drink. I grab my purse from the table where all the *Record* employees still sit around eating and drinking.

I race out of the brewery and catch a cab on my way home. I have something important to do.

Chapter 10: Rory

I 'm in the middle of an executive board meeting with my firm when I get a notification on my phone. I take advantage of a slow moment in the meeting to check the message. It's a text from an unknown number.

I catch one glimpse of the first line of the message.

Hi, Rory. This is Nicole Bates. You may remember that you gave me this number. I hope it's okay for me to contact you.....

I don't read anything else. What the hell does she want now?

This is the first time she's contacted me in more than ten months. I haven't seen or heard from her in all that time except for that one brief incident when I bumped into her at the Castle Brewery.

I sure as hell hope she doesn't take our casual conversation as an invitation to start something up with me. That's the last thing I need now or ever.

She's a reporter. I know better than to think any reporter could want anything from me other than to pry as much information out of me as they can get. She won't be any different. She proved that last time and then some.

I put my phone back in my pocket.

The meeting is one long sequence of slow moments. I could easily check the message and even read it in its entirety, think it over carefully, and decide what to do about it. I wouldn't miss anything important in this meeting. Nothing important happens in the meeting.

I put it off as long as humanly possible before I read the message. I wait until that evening. I'm going out to the bar to meet Niko and Giovanni for drinks and dinner.

Giovanni invited us. He says he needs to get out more, now that he has a wife, a baby, and another one on the way.

Niko says he needs to get out more, too, now that he has his first child at home. Melody doesn't mind if he goes out and talks to other people for a change. She's too tired to think straight and she needs to sleep when she isn't taking care of the baby.

The two of them sit on their side of the table talking about married life and fatherhood. That leaves me as the third wheel, so I pull out my phone to read Nicole's message.

Hi, Rory. This is Nicole Bates. You may remember that you gave me this number. I hope it's okay for me to contact you. I wouldn't bother you except that I think we need to talk. Do you have some time to meet? I can work around whenever is convenient for you. I've been doing some work at the Record *and found out some information that relates to your role as PR officer for The Billionaires' Club. I wouldn't intrude on your time if I didn't think it was important and necessary for me to do so. Please let me know when you can meet. I don't feel right about relaying this information in any other format than in person. It's sensitive in nature and could be volatile if you know what I mean. I hope I hear back from you soon. Thanks in advance for your time.*

I don't know what to think of that. I really don't want to meet her in person, especially not in any capacity related to her work or the club—but at least she was polite about it. I have to give her credit for that.

I don't know what she means about her information being sensitive and potentially volatile. What could that possibly be?

She made it sound at the brewery like she believed in the club and had completely reversed her opinion on it.

Now she makes it sound like she found something that suggests the club is an evil coven of world-dominating masterminds after all. She better not be trying to spin another story like that one.

Meeting her will be the best way for me to head her off at the pass if she is trying to work that angle. Meeting her will be the best way to at least find out which direction she's going. Then I can mobilize the whole club for warfare if I absolutely have to.

I don't want to, but I do have to at least find out.

She thinks it's important and necessary for us to meet so she can divulge this information. She's right about that. It's important and necessary for me to at least find out what this sensitive and potentially volatile information is.

I text her back. *I can make myself available whenever is convenient for you. How about tomorrow night? We can meet back up at the Castle. The* Record *is right around the corner. How about eight o'clock?*

She returns my text in seconds. *That sounds great. I'll see you there. Thank you.*

She's being a lot more polite and professional than I've ever dealt with her before. Maybe she was being sincere about turning over a new leaf. Maybe she really did get the message about how toxically she behaved last time. I can only hope.

I put my phone away and pay more attention to my friends' conversation. I don't know if I'll ever get married and have a family, but I better learn from these guys if I do.

I try to take in as much as I can, but it's kind of hard to relate it to anything concrete when I don't have a wife or a baby at home.

I keep getting distracted by Nicole. This is the second time she's defended the club—and I mean defended it in a big way. She's become one of the club's most vocal defenders—one of the club's only vocal defenders.

I said at the time that the club couldn't be the source of whatever information refuted and debunked her accusations.

Never in a million, trillion years would I have believed that she would reverse herself so completely and so publicly. She really took a dive for us on that one.

I can only respect her for declaring so publicly that she was ashamed of her behavior and lack of journalistic integrity. She really did get it.

Then she did the same thing with this Scott Presley character. She defended the club again—and she went on record doing it.

I just hope she keeps doing it now. I hope that's what she wants to meet me about. I hope she isn't trying to undercut us again.

I get through the rest of dinner with the guys. They both have to go home early and they part on much warmer terms than ever before. Their shared experience of married life and fatherhood brings them closer together.

It leaves me farther behind for exactly the same reason. I have less in common with them now. I wish that wasn't the case, but I couldn't be happier for both of them.

I go home, but Nicole keeps nagging at my mind all evening and all the following day. Our upcoming meeting weighs on me. I really want to find out what it is she thinks is so important.

I get to the Castle early and get us a table. I text her back to tell her where I am.

I stand up when I see her coming toward me. She bursts into a grin while she pulls off her jacket. She's wearing another tight, body-hugging suit. This one is ultra-pale pink—almost white but not quite.

The action of taking her jacket off shows off all her curves. Her chest is stacked to the limit, but she keeps it tasteful by wearing a tight, knitted, short-sleeved sweater underneath her jacket. It makes her look absolutely mouth-watering—but I'm not here to think about that.

Chapter 11: Rory

N icole and I both sit down at the table in the Castle Brewery. "Thanks for meeting me," she breathes and casts a hasty glance around. "I feel like a secret agent infiltrating enemy territory."

I frown at the reference. "What is this about? Why are you being all cloak-and-dagger about this?"

She leans her elbows on the table. "Remember when you said you don't understand why everyone hates the club so much? It made me think and I started to do some digging at the *Record*."

"Yeah? And? Everyone does hate the club. This *Connection* story proves that."

"That's exactly my point, see? Everyone *doesn't* hate the club. They can't, can they, because the club members keep helping so many people. I read an article about Diego Espinosa sending one of his employees' children to college—and they weren't the only family he helped. The same article states that he's bailed out more than fifty of his employees' families when they were in trouble and that he buys Christmas and birthday gifts for his employees, their families, their kids—everyone."

"Yeah? Everyone knows about Diego. He's a prince."

"That's my point. That must be thousands of people—and that's not counting all his charities—and all the charities and people the rest of you have helped. So it isn't possible that everyone hates the club. It's more likely that the people who hate the club are a tiny minority and the people who think the club is great are the majority. That's what I started thinking, anyway."

"So what's your point?" I ask. "What is so important that you needed to meet me in person? You could have told me that in a text. It isn't anything we don't already know."

"Well, you see, Scott Presley told me that he'd already read all of my citations—every single page of every single citation—and he still believed there was something underhanded going on beneath the surface. It got me thinking—so I looked into it."

"And? Is this going somewhere?"

"I wasn't sure, but it turns out that it did go somewhere. It turns out that the same organization owns both news outlets—the *New York Record* and the *Atlantic Connection*. The order to investigate The Billionaires' Club came from the parent company in both cases—in my case and in Scott Presley's case. The parent company gave the order to both editors who passed it down to us the way they usually do."

I stare at her as a prickle of goosebumps runs up my arm. This is big—huge, in fact. She's right. This is a real threat against the club—a much worse threat than I realized.

She's doing me and the club another giant favor—a much bigger, more important favor than just defending us in public. She's going so much further for us than I ever thought anyone could.

She doesn't notice my reaction. She just keeps rattling on giving me more and more and more information.

"Obviously the two editors didn't give us the stories at the same time. The order came down to my editor and then it went to Presley's editor after I published my second story. Whoever sent this order obviously wasn't satisfied that I came to a conclusion that cast the club in a positive light, so our mystery source in the parent company sent out to second order to the *Connection* to look into it and come up with something more damning to refute everything I had already written. Don't worry. I'm still looking into it to find out if the order came from a single individual or from the whole executive or editorial board or what. I thought it was really weird because I was in the middle of my investigation and I hadn't interviewed anyone or even done any research yet. My editor contacted me and demanded that I write the story and send it in so he could print it anyway and then for me to follow up and get the information afterward. That's how I came to write the first piece before I actually found out what the club members were really like. I know I shouldn't have agreed and I shouldn't have sent in the story. I know I did wrong and I'm not trying to excuse myself because there is no excuse. I'm just saying that the pressure was on even then. My editor must have gotten the word to publish the story regardless of what I found out and he managed my investigation that way. I didn't think anything of it at the time because he said he had bumped me up the timeframe and decided to publish the story early to take the place of another story. I accepted that explanation and sent it in because I thought at the time, just like Scott Presley did, that there was no way I could find out anything complimentary about you. So I'm assuming he got the same combination of orders and suggestions and that's what he's doing." She frowns at me. "Are you okay? I just wanted to explain to you what I'm doing and why. I hope you don't think I'm imposing on you by telling you this. I thought you ought to know about it."

I shake myself back to reality. "No, I really appreciate you telling me. You're right. This is critical to the club. Thank you. I owe you one for this."

She sneers at me. "Hardly. I was wondering if I should keep in touch with you after this. I'm still looking into it like I said. I can let you know what I find out. I don't want you to think I'm trying to move into your inbox. I just don't want anyone to smear the club any more than I already have. I feel really bad about the way I acted and the damage I did because of it. You were all so kind to me—especially you. I don't want anyone else to repeat what I've already done. I want to give you whatever information you need to protect yourselves and hopefully stop whoever is doing this."

"I'm.....I'm really grateful to you for doing this, Nicole." God, those words don't even cover how grateful I am. "I would really appreciate it if you kept in touch with me. I don't think you're trying to move into my inbox—not at all. I'm really glad you contacted me about this—and I'm very aware that you took this seriously enough not to use my number for anything less important. I'm glad you did and I want you to do it again. Thank you. I'm sorry I acted defensively when we first got here. I let our previous experience interfere with my expectations. That was a mistake. I hope you can overlook it."

She grimaces at me. "You had every right to think that. I don't blame you. I really wasn't sure if you would see me at all. I wouldn't have been at all surprised if you had turned me down. I would have understood perfectly if you had." She hesitates. "So....what do you want me to do? I was just continuing my research into the parent company. Obviously I can't do this investigation from the *Record* office, so I'm doing it in my free time in the evenings and on the weekends. I don't know how long it will take for me to find the information I'm looking for. It might take a while—but you should tell me if you want me to go in a particular direction or look in a particular place. I'm not sure if you have a particular way you want me to conduct this investigation....."

"You're the expert on that. You should do it whichever way you think is best."

"Are you sure—because I know you're the expert when it comes to the club's public image. I don't want to do anything that will make it harder for you to manage the club's reputation. That's why I'm here. I want you to tell me if you think I'm doing anything or if you want me to handle the information in a certain way to cast the club in the best possible light. That's all I'm trying to do."

I only have to think about it for a split second. "There's no question in my mind that you're trying to cast the club in the best possible light. I think you should run the investigation according to your own judgment and do what you think is best with the information. I trust you."

She stares back at me just as hard. She definitely heard me say that. Maybe now she'll realize that I got the message, too. She changed her whole perspective. She's helping us. She's more than helping us. She's saving us—as surely as I saved her at the gala.

Her expression clears instantly and she bursts into a big, bright, beaming smile. "Okay! I'll do that. Thanks. I wasn't sure what you wanted to do, but I can definitely do it that way." She glances around. "I should probably get out of here."

"Are you sure? Have you eaten? Do you want to get something?"

She beams at me. "I'm all right. Thank you. I better get back to it. I get like a dog with a bone when I'm on a story like this. I just can't let it go until I find out what I want to know. I should get back home and keep digging into this. I don't have a lot of time outside the office when I *can* look into it. I don't want to waste the little time I have—you know? I want to find out what's going on before they strike again. So....I guess I'll contact you when I have something important to tell you—or I'll just handle it on my own depending on what it is. Will that be okay? Are you satisfied with that?"

"Yeah, that would be great. Don't hesitate to call me if you need anything. Okay? I want you to."

She blushes and smiles at me even more broadly. She doesn't look like the hard-boiled investigative journalist who first came after the club.

She looks youthful, idealistic, and fresh in the full flush of her enthusiasm. She's impossibly appealing when she gets like this.

She gathers her jacket, climbs into it so I get a full, unobstructed view of her body arching back and her chest sticking out, picks up her purse, and blushes at me again.

"Have a good evening, okay?" she breathes. "And please don't hesitate to use my number if you find out anything or if you need me to do anything. Please. If something comes up that's relevant to the investigation—or if you want to tell me anything about how you want me to go about it—please don't hesitate to contact me. Okay?"

"Okay. Thank you. Thank you for meeting me. I won't forget this."

"Great," she murmurs. "Good night."

I say, "Good night," and she slides out of her seat. She strides off through the brewery and vanishes into the night.

I don't believe it. I completely misrepresented her. She's so much smarter and her integrity is so much better than I ever gave her credit for. I never thought she could prove herself like this, but she sure is proving herself now.

Chapter 12:
Nicole

I lean back in my chair at my desk in the *Record* news office and read my latest exposé spread out all over the front page. My exposé just isn't spread all over the front page of the *Record*. I had to publish it through alternative outlets.

The year was 1972 and the electronics world was just taking its first steps into what would later develop into the first computers. IBM was in the process of converting its digital card system into the first rudimentary electronics system. Computers, the internet, and cellphones were a long way off, but one man saw the potential and started his own electronics company to try to get ahead of the curve. His name was Vernon Cowan. He wasn't a tech genius by any modern standard. He grew up on a farm in New Hampshire and spent his youth repairing old radios and reselling them to get the money to go to the movies.

He founded Globe Electronics to promote his ideas and inventions to companies he thought might be able to use them. He originally decided to sell his electronics systems to airplane manufacturers, so he called the original company, Globe Aviation Electronics.

Young Vernon wasn't the only person who saw the potential. Globe Electronics caught the attention of two men. They had grown up together in a working-class neighborhood in Philadelphia. One of these men was Curtis McClaren, the robotics genius who would later go on to found Living Robotics, a pioneer in the field that would capitalize on the rollout of robotic automation in automotive factories around the country and later the world.

Those days were still a long way off, too, and at the time, Curtis shared his interest in   Globe Electronics with his best friend, Cain Palmer. Cain worked as an upper level managing executive of Jungle Systems, an analog information aggregator and broker that functioned as a primitive version of the internet. Palmer also saw the potential for using Global Electronics in Jungle Systems.

Both men harnessed the money and influence at their disposal to try to acquire the company for themselves. Neither of the men could afford more than their own basic living expenses at the time, so they both had to leverage huge amounts of debt from their personal finances as well as borrowing from family and friends to come up with the funds to bid on the company.

What had once been a close, supportive friendship quickly disintegrated into one of the worst business feuds between bitter rivals. The competition between the two men became legendary in the business world. Each man tried to establish relationships, build contacts, and bring in outside investment from bigger players in the industry and beyond.

The battle of wills could only end one way. One man would walk away with the spoils while the other would crumble into ruins.

The outcome launched Curtis McClaren to stratospheric success. Global Electronics became one of the foundational technology companies that rode the budding computer development wave to financial stardom. McClaren achieved unbelievable financial success and eventually helped to found The Billionaires' Club we know today.

The competition left Cain Palmer penniless, broken, and unem-
ployed. His attitude toward his work soured until the Board of Trustees
for Jungle Systems sent him packing. He spent three years working as a
used car salesman before he started Capitol Chronicles, *his first news-*
paper.

He eventually achieved success of his own. Capitol Media Group now
owns more than twenty news outlets around the country, including the
New York Record *and the* Atlantic Connection.

Cain Palmer never got over his hatred and resentment for the man
who had once been his best friend. Palmer never achieved the level of
success Curtis McClaren did. Cain Palmer is not a billionaire and
therefore doesn't qualify to join The Billionaires' Club his former friend
helped to establish.

Cain Palmer currently sits on the executive board of Capitol Media
Group. He uses his position to try to undermine and discredit The Bil-
lionaires' Club whenever possible even though the man he hated so much
is long dead.

Cain Palmer originally issued the order to Wayne Grodin, manag-
ing editor of the New York Record, *to investigate the club and dig up*
information on its members to cast the club in a negative light. Cain
Palmer included several talking points and keywords in this order. He
slandered the membership with allegations of misogyny and predatory
behavior against women, illegal business practices, and connections to
organized crime to name just a few.

Grodin passed this order to his journalistic staff, and when the re-
porters involved took too long in their investigation, Palmer issued a sec-
ond order to Grodin to publish the piece anyway without the supporting
evidence to back up his claims.

This story produced the results Palmer wanted. It smeared the club in the public eye and cast the club membership in a negative light to turn public opinion against all billionaires.

There was just one problem. One of the reporters involved got the crazy idea to continue the investigation and found out that all of this innuendo was malicious and unfounded. This reporter discovered that the billionaire club members were not hideous demons from Hell out to suck the lifeblood from those less fortunate than themselves. They were actually good people who used their wealth and success to help as many people as possible. This reporter discovered that the billionaires in the club contributed vast sums of their hard-earned money to charitable causes. Almost all of them had gone out of their way to contribute to the lives of their employees, their employees' families, and even total strangers.

This reporter published a retraction piece that contradicted the narrative Cain Palmer had been trying to create. Palmer struck back by issuing the same order to the editorial staff of the Atlantic Connection. *This order went down to a reporter named Scott Presley. He followed up on all the original source material showing what these billionaires were really doing with their money, but Presley remained convinced that there must be some hidden underlying agenda behind the facts. He reiterated that the billionaires' philanthropic efforts were just a PR spin campaign to cover up their evil machinations behind the scenes.*

Presley published these conjectures without any substantiating references to back them up. The pressure to do this came from Palmer himself. Cain Palmer will continue to use his power and influence to continue this campaign against The Billionaires' Club in whatever news outlets he controls. He'll continue to carry out his vendetta against the organization he hates so much, now that the man he really wants to destroy is no longer around for Palmer to attack directly.

I re-read the story a few different times. I'm proud of my discoveries and I'm proud of the way I presented the information. I'm even proud of the fact that I published it on multiple platforms—none of which are owned by Cain Palmer.

Now the story is all over the internet. Everyone is reprinting it—so Capitol Media Group has no choice but to reprint it, too.

I hope Cain Palmer is sucking on a rotten egg right now. How dare he try to manipulate the news cycle? He doesn't even know anyone in The Billionaires' Club's current membership. He has no reason to single them out for all this venom.

The guy is irrational in his hatred of the club. I can't let him get away with this and I won't let him get away with it. Now everyone knows who he is and what he's doing.

He won't be able to use any of his news outlets to go after the club again—or any of its members. Everyone knows about him now.

Rory will be able to use this story to protect the club. He'll be able to point out if Cain Palmer ever tries to do anything like this again.

I'm proud of myself. I did my job. I acted with journalistic integrity. That's all I need to know.

I switch off my computer and pick up my jacket and purse. I'm just about to go out for lunch when Mael Ronstadt comes up to my desk. He's our clerk. "Wayne is asking to see you in his office, Nicole."

I stiffen—and then relax. I knew this was coming. I couldn't publish a story like this without it producing some ripple effect in the rest of my life.

I published the story expecting Wayne Grodin to fire me from the *Record* journalism staff. I wouldn't be at all surprised if Cain Palmer bans me from working for any other Capitol Media news outlet ever again for my entire career.

I can live with that. I've spent the last week preparing myself for this moment. I'm ready to walk away from this if necessary. I didn't become a journalist so I could attack and ruin good people to satisfy some aging narcissist's vendetta against a dead man.

Chapter 13:
Nicole

I put my jacket and purse back down and head off to Wayne's office. He's an old guy with a white combover and carrying a few too many pounds around his back and midsection.

He peers at me over his glasses when I walk into his office. Then he takes his glasses off. "Shut the door and sit down, Nicole," he murmurs.

I shut the door, but I don't sit down. I want to meet this on my feet. "I'm not going to apologize for this story and I sure as hell am not going to retract it," I tell him. "You put me in a terrible position and pressured me to compromise myself. I shouldn't have let you do that to me. That was my mistake, but you have to admit that you did the wrong thing, too. I'm not going to let you or anyone else continue this campaign against The Billionaires' Club. You can fire me if you want to, Wayne, but no one will ever make me compromise my journalistic standards again—not you, not Cain Palmer, and not anyone else. I'm done. If you can't accept that, then I don't belong at the *Record*."

He heaves an almighty sigh. "No one is planning to fire you, Nicole. I just want you to understand that you put all of us in danger. Cain Palmer is threatening to shut down the whole *Record* because of this."

I blink at him. "Seriously?"

He spreads his hands. "He's talking about closing the *Record* and restarting a completely different outlet under a different name with completely different staff. All of us would be out on the street—not just you. I'm talking about everyone from me and the rest of the editorial staff all the way down to the clerks, janitors, and IT people. Is that really what you want—to put all these people on the unemployment line?"

My temper starts to rise. "You are not pinning this on me! I wouldn't be putting them on the unemployment line—Palmer would! Don't you get that? This is a news outlet, Wayne! Where's your integrity, for Christ's sake?! Our job is to tell the story as factually and accurately as possible—not to do some asshole's dirty work for him! I did my job—that's all! If you have a problem with that, then you're part of the problem and you shouldn't be working in the journalism field at all! None of us should! You and the rest of the *Record* staff should be damn grateful that I published this story through another outlet instead of using my position to put it through the *Record* itself! That's what I should have done! I should have made the *Record* and Capitol Media look as bad as I possibly could—which is what it deserves, Wayne! Jesus! I can't believe we're even having this conversation! We wouldn't be in this situation in the first place if you had done your job and refused to publish the story without checking the facts first. Then we would have printed the second story first and we wouldn't have had to look like the incompetent morons that we are. You should have stood up to him and backed me up—which is what you should be doing now instead of bringing me in here and blaming me for exposing his rotten tactics. Don't you have any self-respect at all? Don't you even care about your commitment to the truth? Is this really why you got into journalism in the first place—because I didn't. I didn't get into journalism to publish a bunch of lies to tear down good people who are doing good things with the success they've worked their asses off to earn. If that is why you got into journalism, then I can walk out of here right now and good riddance because I don't want to work for you, either."

He sighs again. He looks awfully old and tired right now. "That isn't what I got into journalism for, but I do have a job to do in running this operation....."

"Then do it. Do your job and quit wasting my time. Just tell me in one word—do I still have a job here or not—yes or no? That's all I want to hear—one word."

"Yes, you still have a job here."

"Fine. I'll see you later. I have to be somewhere." I storm out of his office fast enough to slam the door against the wall. Good. What a cocksucker. He better not try to twist my arm to retaliate against me for this.

I snatch my jacket and purse and leave the office still fuming. I try to put that conversation behind me, but I'm so mad that I have to stop around the corner, lean against the wall, and take a minute to catch my breath.

I'm all done with this. I will never let anyone step on me again. How dare they?! I mean, what the actual hell?! Did I just fall asleep and wake up in another dimension where the whole profession of journalism means something completely different?

I know a lot of the journalism industry is manipulated by corporate and political interests. I hate to admit that I was one of those people in the past, but I'm not anymore.

Now I actually give a damn about doing my job. Everybody else better get on board with that or get the hell out of my way.

I open my eyes, shake myself, and straighten up. I have things to do. I can't dwell on this anymore.

I'm just about to keep going when my phone rings. I take it out of my purse on my way to the nearest subway station. I stop dead in my tracks when I read the name on the screen. It's Rory Kahn.

I answer it and hold it to my ear with shaking hands. "Hello?"

"Hello, Nicole," he tells me. "It's Rory."

"Hi," I reply. "How are you? Is anything wrong?"

"No, nothing is wrong. I'm just calling you to thank you for your latest piece on Capitol Media. The story is all over the club. Everyone is buzzing about it and they can't stop praising you to the skies for proving yourself to us."

I find myself blushing even though I'm not standing in front of him. "It was the least I could do. I'm glad we could bring the whole thing to a successful conclusion. It's been a long time coming—too long, in fact. It never should have happened in the first place and I'm embarrassed at my involvement in it. I'm just relieved that I could put some of that right and clear the air for all of you."

"Well, thank you. You definitely made up for it and we appreciate it. I was wondering if I could take you to dinner sometime." He hesitates for a split second and then blurts out in a rush, "To say thank you....on behalf of the club."

That moment of hesitation makes me think differently. Is he using this as an excuse to ask me out?

"Is this really on behalf of the club—because I don't want your thanks. Consider this a thank you from me to you—that's all."

"Does it matter if it's on behalf of the club?" he asks. "I'd like to—if you want to."

"Um.....yeah. I'd like that."

"How about eight o'clock Saturday night? I'll pick you up at your place."

Now I know for a fact that he's asking me out. This has nothing to do with the club.

My cheeks turn bright red and I can't help but blush and laugh. "Yeah! That would be great. I'll see you there."

"Great. See you then." He hangs up. I put my phone back in my purse and head for the subway with a spring in my step. I'm going out to dinner with Rory Kahn.

I would have been all a-flutter if some billionaire asked me out before. I can't even think of him as that anymore. He's just Rory. He and I have gone through too much together. He's seen me at my absolute worst and he still wants to go out with me.

He's the one who originally pointed out to me how far off track I was going. He's the one who originally pointed out to me that I had completely abandoned my journalistic integrity.

He was the one who reminded me of who I really am and why I'm doing this. He's a good man and he always acts with integrity no matter what anyone else does.

I don't actually care about his money. I barely even see it anymore—probably because he doesn't act anything like what I expect a billionaire to act like. He's just Rory. He's as solid as they come and he commits himself to doing the right thing for himself and others.

He might not really be asking me out. He might only be doing this on behalf of the club. It doesn't really matter because I really don't want his thanks. I'm not going into this expecting it to be a real date or expecting it to turn romantic.

I'll wait and see if he turns it romantic. I'll have my answer if he doesn't. Then we can both move on and neither of us will have lost anything.

I barely think about him or the club or anything related to the story. The rest of the world loses its collective mind over my exposé, but the furor dies down after a while. We all have better things to do and other stories to work on.

Everyone at the *Record* waits with bated breath for Wayne to fire me. Then everyone sees that he doesn't and the whole subject disappears down the Great Black Memory Hole. Good.

Chapter 14:
Nicole

I leave the office on Friday afternoon, go home, and go through the rest of my weekend. I don't really remember that I'm even going on a date with Rory until noon on Saturday. Even then, I don't really get excited about it or anything like that.

God knows I've talked to him enough times. This will be no different. He asked me at the brewery if I wanted to stick around and get something to eat. That could have turned into a casual social dinner, but it didn't.

He didn't mean it as that. He just wanted to make up for how defensive he acted about me contacting him in the first place.

He's never expressed any interest in me in the past and he still hasn't expressed interest in me by asking me out to dinner. I'm not going to treat this as him expressing interest in me. He'll have to get a lot more explicit about it if he is interested.

I take a long time to decide what to wear tonight. I have no idea where he plans to take me, but he was pretty specific about this being a strictly platonic thank-you dinner.

I dress for that by wearing a light, bluish, eggshell-grey skirt set with matching blazer and white pumps. There. He can't possibly read anything into this outfit. It's dressy enough for just about anywhere he does take me and it doesn't look like I think this is a date.

He shows up at the stroke of eight—of course. As if Rory Kahn would ever, EVER be late for anything.

He shows up in one of his pristine suits. He always wears them, so it isn't like he's treating this as a date, either. I wouldn't be able to tell from his suit if he is treating it as a date.

His eyes make the most fleeting snap down to my outfit the minute I open the door. Now he can see that I'm not implying anything with my outfit, either. We're still on neutral terms here.

I can't help but smile when I see him. "Hi!" I breathe.

"Hi. Are you ready to go?"

"Yeah!" I pull the apartment door shut behind me and we head down the hall toward the elevator. "Where are we going?"

"I made reservations at the Huddlestone Bistro. I hope that's okay."

I nod. "Yeah, I like that place."

His choice of venue doesn't tell me anything, either. The Huddlestone Bistro is an extremely classy and expensive restaurant, but there's nothing particularly romantic about it.

I mean, it could be romantic if we really were on a date, but he probably doesn't mean it that way. Maybe he just wants to take me somewhere classy.

Everything he does is classy, but everything he does is also strictly professional. That's the thing about him. He never expresses anything personal about anything.

Maybe he thinks his personal life is so bad that staying professional would always be an improvement on that—and maybe he's right considering where he comes from.

It doesn't give him much opportunity to get close to people, though. It makes him perfectly smooth and effortless in his dealings with people, but it also creates an impassable barrier to anyone getting close to him.

Maybe that's why he does it. He doesn't want anyone to see what he used to be when he was a homeless street kid living out of dumpsters. I can't blame him for that. I wouldn't want anyone to see that, either, if I had come from there.

I don't want to embarrass him by bringing that up or drawing attention to the fact that I know about his past. I can't imagine why he would be ashamed of it. He ought to be extremely proud of himself.

He's talked openly about his past in interviews before. He's never tried to hide it, so maybe he is proud of it.

He has never revealed the identity of the abusive family he ran away from when he became homeless. He never exposed them or told anyone that they were the ones who abused him. No one knows to this day who they are—except for him. He obviously knows.

He let them continue to draw their stipend from Social Services right up until he turned eighteen while he was living on the street and working to support himself.

I don't bring any of that up on our way down the elevator to the street. I don't plan to mention his background at all. He obviously wants to put it behind him and I'm more than happy to let him do that.

I catch him glancing at me a few times on our way downstairs. I can't help but smile at him when he does. He's so outstanding now the way he is. Why drag up the past that doesn't relate to him anymore?

He eventually breaks the silence. "How have you been? Have you had to deal with much fallout from your story?"

"Oh, you know. Wayne Grodin wasn't happy about it, but it was nothing better or worse than I expected. I prepared myself when I published the story that he would probably fire me."

He spins around fast. "Did he fire you? You didn't tell me that."

"No, no. He didn't. He tried to make me feel guilty about it, but I just stood my ground and pointed out that he was the one who put me in a compromising position by pressuring me to publish an unsubstantiated story in the first place. I told him he was part of the problem and I didn't want to work for him or the *Record* if he wasn't going to at least maintain that minimum standard of professionalism. He dropped it and now everyone has better things to worry about than all of that."

"Wow," he murmurs. "I thought he would fire you, too. I thought Palmer would have been after your neck with an axe."

I find myself laughing. "I did, too, but I guess he can't. Now everyone in the world knows about him. He'll be living under a microscope for the rest of his natural life."

Rory chuckles. "I wouldn't want to be him."

I glance over at him. That's the first time I've ever heard him laugh—about anything.

I don't get a chance to remark on it before the elevator makes it to the ground floor and the doors open. We walk outside to find Rory's black BMW parked at the curb.

The doorman from my building stands there keeping an eye on the car so it doesn't get towed or messed with.

I grin at him when Rory opens the passenger door for me—and finally, finally, he grins back at me. "This is a really cool car," I tell him once he gets behind the wheel and fires up the engine.

"It's great. I always wanted one when I was a kid. It was one of the reasons I really wanted to make a lot of money, so it was one of the first things I bought myself once I made enough to afford it."

That's the first time he's mentioned his past to me, too, but I don't draw attention to that, either.

"Are you the only member of the club who drives your own car?" I ask. "I thought all of you would be riding around in limos."

"Most of them do. A few drive their own cars. Jackson always drives a big black Range Rover. It's like his Terminator-mobile or something. It's the Jackson Metcalf version of the Batmobile."

I laugh. "That's funny. He is a Terminator, isn't he?"

"Lane has a whole collection of exotic cars. He rides around in a limo most of the time, but he goes out driving when he feels like it. It's one of his side passions."

He weaves the car in and out of traffic with expert ease. He drives aggressively like a cab driver, but he never puts us or his precious car in danger. Of course not.

Chapter 15:
Nicole

R ory pulls up in front of the Huddlestone Bistro, lets me out, and hands his keys to the valet. The guy's eyes widen when he gets into the car.

"You are never going to see that car again," I tell Rory. "Say goodbye now."

He laughs at that, too. He actually laughs out loud this time. "Hush your mouth, girl."

He leads the way inside and the host seats us at a table to one side. It's quieter over here, but still not overtly romantic.

"So what's going on with the club?" I ask. "You said everyone was losing their minds over my story."

"Not the story so much. Mostly just over you."

My head shoots up. "Me?! Why?"

"Just because none of us ever expected you to go that far to prove yourself. None of the others even saw the story until I pointed it out to them."

I blink at him in shock. "You pointed it out to them."

He nods. His eyes speak volumes. "I actually brought it up at a general meeting. I put it on the agenda so they would all see it and I could let them know that you were the one who wrote the piece. I know you don't want us thanking you or anything like that, but I wanted all of them to understand how completely you reversed yourself since the gala. That was the least you deserved after the risk you took for us."

I look away. I don't like hearing him talk about me like this.

"You did a great thing," he murmurs. "Let us appreciate it for what it was. You told me once that I didn't have to keep locking myself away and you don't, either. You don't have to keep doing penance for your past behavior. You balanced the scales. You can start over with a clean slate. It's done. We're even."

I look up to find him gazing into my eyes with a much deeper level of meaning and compassion. He hasn't looked at me like this since that night at the hospital.

"Thanks," I croak. "That's all I was trying to do."

"You did. You redeemed yourself beyond any of our expectations. Everyone in the club respects you for that. So let us respect you for it. No one in the club thinks you're a scumbag anymore. We all think you're a good, honest reporter committed to the facts. We trust you because you've proven yourself trustworthy. Accept it and be happy about it. Let us say thank you. That's all you have to do."

I feel my cheeks burning. I find it hard to look at him when he gets that expression on his face. "Thank you....I mean....you're welcome."

He laughs again and the waiter comes to give us our menus. He also brings a bottle of wine. Is this supposed to be Rory's way of turning the dinner romantic? He still doesn't give any indication of that.

He keeps looking deep into my eyes across the table, but it's his understanding, compassionate, searching look. I don't see anything romantic in it.

He pours for both of us and raises his glass. "Here's to clean slates, new beginnings, fresh starts, and all of that."

I smile at him. "Yeah. Here, here." We both take a sip. "So what's the new beginning for you?"

"Do you mean apart from not having to worry about Palmer coming after the club? I don't know. It seems like....." He trails off.

I realize my mistake instantly. "Don't tell me if it's too personal."

He studies me with a very different expression on his face. "I don't know if I should tell you—not because it's you, but because saying it out loud would make it real somehow. I don't know if I'm ready for that."

I stare at him in shock. "Maybe you shouldn't tell me if it's that big."

He shrugs. "It's interesting. I'm one of the youngest men in the club. The young guys always used to have this kind of separate club within the club where we were sort of like the wild and reckless bunch that never took life too seriously. Giovanni was the only one who really did it that way. The rest of us were as serious as anyone, but we and everyone else had this idea that we were somehow as wild and reckless as he was even though we weren't. Now they're all married and settling down. I can't think of anyone more serious than Giovanni is now. The club within the club isn't there anymore—or if it is, it's changed into the exact opposite of what it used to be. Now I'm the only man in that group who isn't married with kids or at least some on the way."

I can't stop gaping at him across the table. Is he really talking to me...about *this*?

I don't know what to say. "You're one of the most serious people I've ever met. I don't think anyone could see you as wild and reckless—not ever."

"That's my point. I'm not. I never have been. Niko hasn't ever been, either. He and I used to be the old men of that group. We were the ones trying to steer all these young players down the path of righteousness as it were. Now it's almost like the other way around."

"It can't be!" I point out. "No one has to steer *you* down the path of righteousness. That's absurd!"

He shrugs again and frowns into his wine glass. "Maybe the path of righteousness I need to be steered down isn't the path of being serious and exact in my business. Maybe the path of righteousness is being a husband, father, and part of the wider community—like the older guys are. Maybe that's where I'm failing and falling behind while all these formerly reckless players grow up and leave me in the dust."

My stomach drops. He is not talking to me about this. I can't believe what I'm hearing.

I gulp trying to come up with something to say to that, but fortunately, the waiter comes right then to take our orders. Rory and I both use the opportunity to pretend that he didn't just reveal something so personal and sensitive.

I never would have believed he could talk to me about something like this. What should I say? No way in hell will I ask what he plans to do about this or if he plans to start looking for someone to settle down with or anything like that.

Am I supposed to read into this that he considers me in that category? I would have expected him to say so if he was.

I did ask what the new beginning was for him. He answered my question. That's all.

"What about you?" he asks after the waiter leaves. "What's next for you? Do you think you'll keep doing journalism forever? Are you married to the job?"

There's that word again. Is he trying to drop a hint or did that word just happen coincidentally in conversation?

I find myself shrugging too much, too. "I wouldn't say I'm married to the job. It's a living—which everyone needs, don't they? I like the job and it pays well, so I guess I have no reason not to keep doing it until something else comes along."

"You seem passionate about it—at least, you do since you committed yourself to doing it the right way. What you just said about standing up to Wayne Grodin—that sounds like you're passionate about it."

"I am. I just wouldn't say I'm so committed to it that I would sacrifice the rest of my life to it. It's a great job and I love it, but it's still a job. It isn't my reason for existing. If something came up that I was more interested in or more passionate about or that I felt more called to do, then I would do that instead. That's the reason—not journalism itself if that makes any sense."

"Yeah, it does. It makes a lot of sense."

"How about you? Is that the way you feel about PR?"

"PR is my area of expertise. It's what I do best and it's what the world most wants from me. That's why I do it—because the world wants me to. It's the vehicle by which I can give people the most of what they need and want at any given moment. It's kind of like my position in the club. PR is the only tool I have at my disposal to give back to the club and use my skills in a way that everyone else needs me to. The club would have to hire a company to do our PR if I didn't do it. I can do it as well as any company we might hire if not better, so doing it for them is my way of doing my part. I'm the only one of the young guys who serves as an officer, so it's an honor for me to be part of that group. It's a win-win as far as I'm concerned—and I guess you could say I see my whole business that way. The client wins by getting the best possible service and I win by making my living at it."

"You're doing a lot better than just making a living." I take that moment to launch into the question that's been burning a hole in the back of my mind ever since I first met him. "Why do you live in such a modest apartment if you aren't locking yourself away? Why don't you let yourself experience nice things the way the others do? You gave yourself that car. Why don't you give yourself the luxury of a nicer place to live?"

"I never attached my living place to success the way I did to the car. Maybe it's because I'm a guy and the car is an expression of manhood for me—or something like that."

I laugh. "Let's hope and pray it isn't that."

He grins back at me. "The car is a trophy. It's a sign that I accomplished what I set out for myself to accomplish."

"Didn't you want a nice place to live when you were younger? I can't believe that."

He doesn't miss a beat that we're talking about his past. He must have realized a long time ago that I would find out about him.

"Of course I did and I got that. I have a very nice place to live. It's everything I ever wanted and much more. I'm comfortable there and I don't attach success to having a colossal mansion many hundreds of times too big for one person to live in. I don't make any judgments on the other guys if that's the way they want to do it, but I don't need that. It would be too much for me when I'm by myself. Maybe I would feel differently if I had a houseful of kids the way Jackson does. It makes more sense when he actually needs the space for a family his size."

I guess I can't argue with that. I have no experience of having that kind of money.

"Where are you from?" he asks. "You obviously know enough about me."

I squirm in my seat. "I'm from Manhattan. I grew up here."

His eyebrows fly up. "Really? What a shock."

I laugh. "I know, right? I don't know anyone else who is from here—except my dad, of course."

"Do you have other family here?"

"He still lives here. My mom died when I was eleven and my two older brothers are both married with children. One of them lives in Jersey and works over there, so my dad and I go down there to visit him for holidays and whatnot. My other brother lives on the West Coast and he comes over here to have holidays and whatnot in Jersey, too, so it's just me and my dad holding down Manhattan for posterity."

He laughs again. He seems genuinely delighted that we're talking so much more openly and more comfortably than before. This feels good. It feels like we could actually be social acquaintances instead of holding each other at a professional distance.

The waiter comes with our food just then and we start eating. I don't feel uncomfortable eating in front of him, now that we've thawed the ice.

Eating with him feels like eating with a social acquaintance or maybe even a friend. Maybe we could get to that point someday if we keep talking like this. Tonight was a step in the right direction.

He drives me home afterward and walks me back inside to my apartment door. We turn and face each other in the hall outside.

Now I know for sure that he won't make any romantic overtures toward me. I don't know if tonight was strictly a thank-you on behalf of the club. Maybe he wanted to test the waters to find out if anything would develop between us.

He won't kiss me or hold my hand or do anything to express interest in me. I can accept the situation between us as that and only that. We're acquaintances getting to know each other better. It doesn't have to be anything more than that.

I respect him and appreciate him for the person that he is. I admire that he can talk so freely about his past and how it relates to the way he does things now.

"I had a really nice time tonight," I tell him. "Thank you for taking me out. It was a pleasure to get to know you better—and I really appreciate you wiping the slate clean."

"You did that. You did that all by yourself."

"Well, I still appreciate it. I appreciate being able to start over with no hard feelings."

"Definitely not. I had a nice time tonight, too. I like talking to you. Can I take you out again?"

I take a split second to realize what he just said. He isn't asking on behalf of the club. It isn't about that anymore. This is definitely about him and me.

"If you want to go out again," I reply, "maybe you would let me take you out somewhere."

His eyes fall out of their sockets. "Really? Uh....okay. Thank you."

I grin at him. "Great. How about next Saturday?"

He laughs. "Are you going to pick me up at my place in your car?"

I turn bright red. "You can pick me up in yours. I'm sure yours is much nicer—because I don't have a car."

His cheeks color. He won't stop grinning in genuine delight. God damn, he is gorgeous when he smiles like that!

"Okay," he murmurs. "Eight o'clock Saturday. Be there—I mean here."

I laugh. "Yeah. You, too. Don't be late or there will be consequences."

We both laugh. "Good night," I tell him.

"Good night."

I go inside and shut the door so he has no choice but to leave. Yay! We're going out next Saturday night.

Chapter 16: Rory

I have absolutely no idea what to expect when I pull up to Nicole's building on Saturday night. I'm still not sure if our last dinner was a date or not, but this definitely is.

I don't know what to think about her asking to take me out. This could turn into something I would rather not get involved with, but it sure looks like I'm about to find out.

I find myself getting nervous on my way upstairs. I don't know what this is that's going on between us, but something definitely is.

I opened up to her a lot more last time than I initially planned to. I can't remember in hindsight if I even had a plan, but it wasn't that. I didn't really plan to hold her at a distance for the rest of eternity, but I planned to do it a lot longer than I did.

Something about the way this whole thing makes me confide in her. I don't really have to because she already understands pretty much everything about me.

I mean, she understands everything that's on record. I don't have to explain about that. I do have to explain what I'm thinking now. She doesn't know that and she won't know if I don't tell her.

She's the only person alive I've told about the way things are going for me in the club. I still can't explain to myself why I told her that, but I don't regret it.

I guess that's the part I didn't expect—that I trust her enough to confide in her about stuff like that—stuff I would never tell any other living soul.

I knock on her apartment door and she opens it. She doesn't show up wearing one of her skirt outfits this time.

She wears a mid-length, above-the-knee white dress with a slight flare downward from the narrow waist. The dress ends with a pretty bell-shaped flower skirt at the bottom.

She slithers through the door on white heels with a white sequined purse. She looks charming, subtly gorgeous, and definitely dressed up for a date. She doesn't look like we're platonic acquaintances any-more—just in case I left her in any doubt about that last time.

"Ready?" I ask.

She blushes. "Yeah! Are you ready to go get into my car and drive across town?"

I laugh. "What is it—a Maserati?"

She turns red and beams at me. "I was thinking more of a Bentley."

"Perfect. Let's go."

I want to take her hand in the elevator on the way downstairs, but I don't want to act too forward too fast. This is technically our first date—our first real date. The others don't count. They were just warm-ups.

I open the passenger door for her to get into my car. She catches my eye and we both laugh.

"Where are we going?" I ask once I start the engine.

"Head down Fifth Avenue," she tells me.

I turn out onto the street. "I can't wait to see where you're taking me. This is a whole new experience—having a girl take me out."

"Don't lie. You don't go out with girls at all, do you?"

"No, you're right."

"Have you ever gone out with girls—like ever?"

"Sure...a few times. I went out with a few before I started my own business. I haven't taken anyone out since then. The two didn't seem to mix."

"What about now? Do you still feel that way?"

"I guess it would be more accurate to say that casual dating like that didn't mix with running my business—and it still doesn't. I didn't articulate it to myself then because I didn't put the pieces together then. I didn't put the pieces together at all until recently, but it doesn't seem like running my business mixed with anything that wasn't serious. I wasn't serious, so it didn't mix. That's why I didn't do it. I didn't think about it. I told myself I was too busy or whatever. I didn't connect the dots until recently."

She doesn't ask if I consider us serious. We aren't asking those questions—not yet.

I drive downtown until we get closer to Washington Square. "Turn onto 8th Street," she tells me.

I turn and then she directs me onto Mercer Street. "I'm dying of curiosity," I mutter.

"Keep going and take a left onto Canal Street."

I frown at her, shake my head, and make the turn. I keep casting frowning glances at her on the way down Canal Street, but she gives nothing away. This isn't the kind of upscale neighborhood I would have taken her if I was the one taking her out.

She points to the left. "Turn here."

I turn off onto Elisabeth Street and then she points right. "Park here."

I pull into a cramped, dirty, deserted alley. My car looks lightyears out of place. I'm not sure I feel right about leaving my car here unattended, but I decide to put my faith in her. She seems to know where she's going—at least I hope she does. She better.

I can't help scowling at the surroundings when I get out and open her door for her. We both get out in the alley and I set the alarm on my car just in case.

"This way," she tells me and climbs down a set of concrete stairs leading into the basement. She walks through a solid steel door that looks like it came from an ironworks factory.

She holds the door open for me to enter behind her. The door opens into a dining room full of small, round tables, each with a single candle burning in the center. Some of the tables have two chairs on opposite sides. Other tables have four chairs.

A pristine white cotton tablecloth covers each table. A cloth napkin folded into an upright origami lotus occupies the spot next to each spotless water glass and wine glass. All the silver cutlery shines in the dim light.

She leads the way to one of the tables. She and I are the only people in here. The steamy, delicious smell of spicy, savory food assaults our noses the minute we walk in.

"I'm guessing you don't want me to pull out your chair for you," she murmurs under her breath.

I make a face and step around the table to pull hers out for her. She smiles at me when I do that and she sits down. I sit down opposite her.

"This is absolutely not what I was expecting at all," I tell her.

"I'm glad I could surprise you. This place has the best food in all of New York. I promise you that."

"I'm sure it does." I frown at the room again. "How did you find out about this place?"

She opens her mouth to answer, but right then, the elderly owner comes out of the kitchen. He wears a white apron over his clothes.

He's wearing a suit, but without his jacket on. He even wears his shirt sleeves buttoned down to his wrists.

He holds out his arms when he sees Nicole and launches into a tirade of rapid Italian. She gets to her feet, hugs him, and kisses him on the cheek while she greets him and answers him in the same fluent river of perfect Italian. I stand up and wait for them to finish.

The owner holds her at arm's length and bombards her with questions in Italian. She waves back and forth between him and me. "Rory Kahn, this is my father, Vitale Gerace. Papa, this is Rory Kahn. He's taking me out on a date tonight."

Her father extends both hands to me and clasps my hand in both of his. "A pleasure, a pleasure!" he gushes in a heavy accent. "It's always a pleasure to meet the gentleman who takes out my Nicolina. Please—sit down. You should have only the best."

"Would you mind bringing Rory a menu, Papa?" she asks.

"Of course, of course—unless you want to order for him." He bursts out laughing, jabs his elbow at me, and goes into the kitchen. He comes back with a menu, opens it in front of me, and points at something. "This is the house specialty for tonight. It's the best!" He kisses his fingertips.

"Stop messing around, Papa!" she tells him. "Get out of here and go back to work!"

He laughs even more loudly, grins at her, and raises his eyebrows several times in a suggestive way before he leaves me and Nicole alone.

Chapter 17: Rory

Nicole and I both sit back down at the table in her father's restaurant. "Don't eat what he told you to," she tells me. "You can get anything else, but not that. He's just having fun."

I lean across the table and lower my voice to a confidential murmur. "This? Seriously? You brought me here....because your father owns this restaurant?"

"You asked how I knew about this place. I know about you. Now you know about me. My father supported me and my brothers on his own by running this restaurant. My father put all three of us through college with this restaurant. My brothers and I grew up working here to help put food on the family table. This is my life right here. I know about you. Now you know about me. That's why I brought you here—because I want you to know the truth about me. I don't want you to think I grew up in some brownstone on the Upper East Side."

I cast another frown at the room and shake my head over the menu. "Wow. I mean...just wow. I'm dumbfounded."

"I grew up believing in the American Dream. I never saw it in action until I found out about The Billionaires' Club—and you. You're a perfect example of that—and I guess I am, too. That's what I wanted you to see. I wanted you to see where I came from and how I got where I am."

I find myself staring at her. She is absolutely not what I expected at all. I really did think she grew up in a brownstone on the Upper East Side. I never in a million years would have guessed she could come from somewhere like this.

I take a split second to make my decision and extend my hand across the table. She stares at it lying open in front of her. Then she turns bright red and puts her hand in it for me to hold.

She won't look up to make eye contact with me. She keeps glancing at our hands and looking away.

Her hand sends a rush of exhilaration up my arm. My heart seizes and adrenaline burns my stomach that I'm holding her hand like this. She feels electric and at the same time soft, sensual, and vulnerable.

"You're beautiful," I murmur. "You're a hundred times more beautiful to me because of this. Thank you for bringing me here. You have no idea what an honor it is to meet your father."

She makes a face. "He's a practical joker. He'll try to catch you out no matter what you do. He doesn't mean anything by it. It's his way of trying to be friendly."

I find myself beaming at her. "Thank you for the warning. I'm going to have to rely on you to help me avoid an ambush."

She laughs. She won't stop blushing. Holy crap, she is beautiful!

I feel so much closer to her right now. Gratitude overflows my heart that she trusts me this much.

"This is the best date I've ever been on," I tell her. "Thank you so much for bringing me here."

She finally glances up and her eyes twinkle with mischief. "Would you like me to order for you?"

"I think you better." I shut the menu. "I am obviously way out of my depth here."

"Don't worry. I'll protect you from the locals."

"Where is everyone?" I ask. "Why don't more people come in for dinner?"

"It's hit and miss. He used to have an extremely dedicated customer base of hardcore fans. They would come in almost every night. It used to take all four of us working nonstop just to keep up with demand. This place would be packed from the minute he opened the doors with a line of people waiting to get a table. He would have to drive people away when we closed at night. That was my life for years. My brothers and I used to come home from school, scramble to change our clothes, and eat dinner before we had to come work at the restaurant for the evening. We used to do our homework at the dinner table because we wouldn't have time to do it later. Then we would come down here and it would be all on until ten or eleven at night. Then we would have to help Papa do the dishes, clean up the kitchen, and put all the leftover food away so we could do it all again the next night. We did that seven nights a week for years—right up until my brothers and I left home."

"So what happened to all the business?"

She shrugs. "I guess some of his customers got old and died—or their kids who knew about this place moved away. Things changed. Not as many of the old people stuck around for one reason or another and new people didn't find out about the place quickly enough. Things have been dropping off, but he still gets enough people to stay in business and support himself. He loves this place. He'll never stop working. He wouldn't know what to do with himself if he did—and he's really close to all his customers. They're family. They all love him to pieces and he loves them. We grew up considering all the customers family. They kept us going when my mom died."

"That is an amazing story," I tell her. "I'm proud of you—and your whole family. It's a story for the record books."

"So is yours. You should be extremely proud of yourself."

"I am. I couldn't be happier with the way things turned out."

I find her studying me across the table. The look in her eyes makes me stroke my fingers across hers. That satin sensation of her touch makes my heart stop. I've never felt this way about anyone.

My touch seems to make her uncomfortable. She looks away.

"Does it bother you—me holding your hand like this?" I ask. "I can stop if you want me to."

"No, it doesn't bother me." Her voice strains. She can barely get the words out.

I squeeze her hand tighter and lower my voice to match hers. "Look at me, Nicole."

Her eyes dart up to meet mine and she immediately looks away.

"What's wrong? Did I do something to offend you by holding your hand like this?"

She opens and closes her mouth several times before she finds the voice to make herself heard. "You just.....I don't know.....you looked at me like that....in the hospital..."

Those words make my blood run cold. I don't know why I had somehow convinced myself that we would never mention that night.

I refuse to let go of her hand. She'll have to take her hand away if she doesn't want us to hold hands. I won't let go first.

I massage and stroke her hand a little tighter. I don't want to stop. This means too much. "You were beautiful that night—and I don't mean when I found you in the bathroom. I mean afterward when you finally got it that we weren't the monsters you thought we were. You were beautiful because you let me see you—just like you're letting me see you now. I don't want whatever superficial façade you think the rest of the world wants to see. I want to see you for real—like I'm seeing you right now." I press her fingers and run my thumb across her knuckles. "If I like you at all, it's because of this."

"I know," she squeaks. "That's what I want. I just.....it's scary.....to think someone could actually like me for this."

"I do like you for this. You should be extremely proud of where you come from. You shouldn't try to hide it. You said I should be proud of where I come from and so should you. Your story is just as impressive as mine. Isn't that why you brought me here—so I would know you for who you really are?"

She starts to nod, but her father comes back right then. She pulls her hand back like she doesn't want him to see us holding hands.

She launches into another long explanation in Italian of what she wants him to bring for both of us. He won't stop grinning at her and shooting knowing glances at me.

He makes eye contact with me as if I can understand what they're talking about and we share some secret about his daughter.

His expressions and body language make me like him instantly. He seems like a genuinely friendly, fun-loving guy even if we have a language barrier.

She says something that makes him burst out in loud, belly laughs. He takes the menu away from me, answers her, and leaves us alone.

Chapter 18: Rory

I wait, but Nicole doesn't put her hand back out for me to hold. She keeps squirming in her seat over there and won't look at me.

I should probably leave it alone, but everything she's done tonight and everything she is just won't let me drop it. I hold out my hand again and she takes it. She leaves it there so we can hold hands across the table.

The fact that she's so nervous charms me even more. She's absolutely priceless. I wouldn't have her any other way. Maybe she's just unnerved that someone is seeing her so unguarded like this. I'm probably the only guy she's ever brought here.

I take a long time to decide what to say to her. I should talk to her and put her at ease.

"You said your dad was from Manhattan," I begin and then I remember. "How did you wind up with the name Bates? Why don't you have your dad's last name?"

"My mom....she *was* a rich princess from the Upper East Side." She makes a face at the reference—again. She wants me to understand that she isn't a princess from the Upper East Side. "Her parents had a heart attack when they found out she was in love with a poor grocer's son from Little Italy. They thought every Italian in the neighborhood was a mobster. They refused to meet him and they threw my mom out with nothing but the clothes on her back when she said she wanted to marry him. They got married anyway and she moved in with him and his parents in their tiny apartment...." She points up and to the left. "Right over there. He had three brothers—all older. They moved out and my parents inherited the apartment when my grandparents died. We all grew up in that apartment."

"So do your uncles still live in the neighborhood?"

"Not in this neighborhood. They all moved up and out, but they still live in Manhattan—all but one. He died when he was in his twenties—but the other two are here with their families."

"So you were telling me about your last name."

"Oh, yeah." She's warming up now. Good. "My parents decided to give me and my brothers her last name—to avoid the kind of prejudice he got from her parents. I guess it was a lot worse back then. They thought we would suffer and people would jump to conclusions if they heard that we had an Italian last name—and maybe they were right. I don't know. Anyway...yeah. It's my mom's last name. That's the story behind it."

"And you never had anything to do with your mother's family? That's tragic."

I shrug. "You don't miss what you never had." She glances up at me and looks away. "Sorry. I shouldn't have said that."

"Hey! Stop apologizing." I squeeze her hand. "I want you to feel free to ask me anything—literally. If you want to know something about me, just ask. I have no secrets from you. I wouldn't be here if I did."

She finally looks up. "What happened to your family?"

"I have no idea. I was already in the foster system by the time I was old enough to remember anything. No one ever told me what happened to them."

"Didn't you feel even slightly curious to find out?"

"Not really. I had bigger fish to fry just figuring out where my next meal was going to come from. Then I got older and it just didn't seem to matter anymore. I wouldn't know if I met one of them on the street."

"That's kind of sad, isn't it?"

"You don't miss what you never had. I was too glad to get away from anything with the word, 'family' attached to it."

"That really is sad. I wouldn't want to live without family."

"I can understand why considering where you come from." I look around the empty restaurant. "You have a beautiful family. I can see that."

Her eyes bore into my depths. This is the deepest she's looked at me so far. Then she glances down at our hands again.

"What's wrong?" I ask. "What's bothering you?"

"I don't know." Her voice breaks. "I just never let myself believe it could come to this. I didn't think.....I didn't think you were that interested in me."

"I wasn't. I wasn't even remotely interested in what I saw in you before. Things are different now because I see you as a completely different person." I take a deep breath and dive right in. "I'm not sure if you're uncomfortable about me seeing you like this, but this is what makes me interested in you. You weren't someone I *could* be seriously interested in before. Now you are."

"I guess I just didn't prepare myself for things to go this far this fast."

"We can back off if you want to. We don't have to hold hands."

"No!" She puts a very slight amount of additional pressure on our hands. Holy crap, her hand fells so good. "I want to."

"Nicole....look at me...."

Her eyes snap to my face and lock on me with brutal power. That look sends another jet of fire through my insides.

"Look at me…" I breathe. "Don't look away."

Her features convulse when she finally lets herself see me staring back at her. She's right. I see her the way I saw her at the hospital. She was vulnerable and hurt then—and not because some cocksucker tried to assault her in a hotel bathroom.

She was vulnerable and hurt because meeting us at the gala wrecked her world. That meeting tore her world down around her ears until she had nothing left. She let me see her like that—or I was the one who was there to see it.

She let me take care of her that night. I was the one who found her and saved her from that guy. I was the one who saw her half-undressed and now I'm sitting here with her in her father's restaurant.

"Who knows about this?" I ask. "And you? Who have you told besides me?"

"No one," she replies. "No one at work knows. A few people from my high school knew. Their parents came here and brought the kids with them, so they found out. I haven't told anyone since."

"Are you ashamed of it?"

"No, not at all. I guess I just felt like…you know….that it was too special and I didn't want to share it with just anyone. I didn't want to put it on the internet or anything like that, you know? I figured I would tell someone if it became important for me to…..which is what I did."

Those words stab me in the heart again. She feels that way about me—just like I'm starting to feel that way about her. She thinks I'm special. She thinks *we're* special.

I think she's pretty special, too. I think she was absolutely right to save this for someone she thought really needed to know.

I'm that person. I'm the person she wants to really know her. She doesn't give a crap about the people at work or whatever guys she's been going out with. She obviously never considered any of them important enough to share this side of herself with them.

I wish I could give her something equally important to me, but she already knows everything about me. Everyone does. It isn't a secret.

I can't stop squeezing and rubbing her hand. She's unimaginably special to me. I never thought our second date would turn into this.

Chapter 19: Rory

Nicole's father comes back to our table before I have a chance to say anything else to her. He comes out of the kitchen balancing an enormous tray on the fingertips of his left hand and carrying some kind of folding stand in the other.

He moves the tray around like some kind of circus master, but he never spills anything. He unfolds the stand next to our table, puts the tray down on it, and starts unloading an absolute metric crap-ton of food onto the table in front of me and Nicole.

He serves each of us a massive plate of food and then piles the table with more and more and more side dishes, appetizers, and God only knows what else. I don't even recognize half of this stuff.

She thanks him in Italian. I thank him in English. He beams at me and leaves.

"Is it safe to eat now?" I ask. "Jesus, he doesn't really expect us to eat all of this, does he?"

"No, of course not. He always gives people enough to take home with them."

I frown at the food in front of me and poke it with my fork to make sure it isn't still alive. "What is this?"

She laughs at me. She's much more at ease now. "It's coda alla vaccinara." I have a hard time keeping up with her when she speaks Italian. "It's a Roman specialty."

"Should I be worried?"

She laughs at me. "Just eat it. It's oxtail braised in tomato and red wine. It's delicious. I wouldn't have ordered it for you if it wasn't."

I can only trust her, so I taste it. She's right. It tastes mind-blowing. I start eating and she shoots me a grin across the table.

"Should I ask what you're having?" I ask.

"Probably not."

"Fair enough. Maybe you can educate me."

She grins again. "Let's start with the basics first."

"So......" I change my mind and don't ask what I was just about to ask. That would really freak her out.

"What?" she asks. "Go on. You want me to ask you anything. Spit it out."

"Did you help your father cook in the kitchen?"

She nods. "All the time. My brothers and I had to take over for him if he ever got sick. We had to learn everything he knows."

I look down at my plate and then turn my attention to the side dishes. "I might have to be intimidated by that."

"Why? Don't you know how to cook?"

"No. I'm hopeless."

"Did you never have the opportunity to learn?"

"Not when I was a kid. I survived on fast food when I got old enough to afford to buy food for myself. I eat better these last several years, but it's just too convenient to buy food already made. I don't have time to cook for myself or any reason to take the time to learn. I buy specialty meals that are really healthy and nutritious. Cooking for myself has always been a luxury I don't really need to take the time to learn."

"I guess that makes sense." She takes a mouthful of her food and pulls one of the side dishes toward herself. It's a bunch of tiny folded dumpling things smothered in cheesy sauce.

She serves half of them onto her own plate and the other half onto mine. It looks like I'm eating this, too.

I stick one of the dumplings in my mouth. Okay, it's official. I officially trust her to pick out my food.

She sees my reaction and laughs at me again. "That's right. Enjoy yourself," I tell her. "I'm happy to be your guinea pig."

She snorts and chokes on....whatever it is she's eating over there. Now I'm the one who gets to laugh at her while she drinks her water and blows her nose.

We somehow finish the meal and get ready to leave with two enormous paper bags full of extra food. "You should take this," I tell her.

"Uh-huh," she counters. "This is all you."

"Are you at least going to tell me what this stuff is?"

"You have the internet. Do your research. Where's your journalistic integrity?"

I laugh. I don't let her see how much I tip her father when I sign the credit card receipt.

I'm relieved to find my car still in the same place and still intact with the wheels attached when I take her outside. I let her into the passenger seat and start the motor, but this isn't the way I want the evening to end.

I extend my hand across the seat and she takes it. She won't stop smiling at me and her cheeks flush. I'm finally sitting close enough to her that I can lean across the seat, slip my fingers into her hair, and kiss her. She melts into me.

I slow way down when I start to kiss her. She feels blissfully, magically, hypnotically soft. I kiss her extra gently and let our lips explore each other deeper as that kiss builds in depth and emotion.

I shut my eyes and kiss her all the way down to her beautiful secret soul. I kiss the part of her that no one else has seen—the part she wants me to see.

I kiss her for showing me that and introducing me to the part of her life that's too special and important for her to share with anyone else. I feel like I'm kissing the person I saw at the hospital—the hurt, ashamed, wronged part of her that only I get to see.

She kisses me back as gently and sweetly as I could hope. She's so exquisite. Her mouth opens and her tongue joins with mine in the dark swirl of everything I feel about her.

We both pull away at the same time. I keep my hold on her hand and drive one-handed back out onto the street to take her home.

It's already late, so I park in front of her building and hold her hand on the way up the elevator. I stop her outside her apartment door. I don't even know what to say to her. The way I feel about her is starting to get the better of me.

I want to say so many things to her. I want to ask her if she's going to cook for me like that after we get married—but I don't want to jump the gun. I can always ask that later. I don't need to rush.

I really don't want to leave. I want to keep standing here looking at her and have her look at me. Her gaze justifies me somehow. She's proud of me—as proud as I am of her. She sees me for who I am and it's okay. Her gaze gives me something I didn't know I needed.

She squeezes my hand once. "I guess this is good night."

"Yeah," I murmur and I take a step forward to kiss her.

She sinks into me—and our kiss erupts into something so much more than before. I can't explain why. The heat explodes off the charts the minute our lips meet.

This isn't a sweet, gentle, tender kiss of deepest emotion. It's a scorching torrent of blistering, ravenous passion.

Kissing her lights my body on fire and I instantly start getting hard when I feel her tongue. Her tongue spirals through my mind setting off one detonation of molten power after another. I can't stand this.

I try to keep my distance so she won't feel me burning up for her, but she comes at me just as hard. She must be reacting to me the way I'm reacting to her.

She wraps her arms around my neck. I can't keep my hands off her. I grab her with both arms around her waist and lift her off the floor so I can devour her mouth with everything I have.

She pants into my nose and her smell sends me into a delirious, drunken frenzy. I turn sideways for some reason. I spiral out of my mind just from kissing her.

Her lips infect me with so much raging hunger for her. I can't get through tonight without having her—but I can't. I don't want to step on her toes.

Her body trembles with so much tension. I have to fight myself not to grope her all over right this minute. She shudders when I crush her against me—and then I feel her soft breasts pressing into my chest.

My arms circle her narrow waist and that shiver of excitement rushes down her thighs. I get one mental flash of the sensual darkness between her legs. I can't let myself go there—not like this.

I try to put her down and we both lose our balance. She's hugging me around the neck too tightly and we both stagger into the wall. I fall on top of her, get one instantaneous charge that I'm lying on top of her, and rear away to stop myself.

She holds onto me tightly enough and kisses me deeply enough not to notice anything wrong until we both topple sideways and she lands on top of me against the wall. She squeals when my knee winds up sticking between her legs and she falls on top of that.

She pulls away, but only for a second. Both of our eyes snap open and I see her staring back at me from inches away. Our lips stay locked together right up until that moment.

That moment of eye contact breaks the spell. We're both so turned on that the incident changes in a flash. She rides down on my leg on purpose this time and her eyes blur out of focus as an unstoppable wave of erotic passion sweeps down her to her hips.

She undulates her body against me, feels how raging hard I am, and arches her hips down to tease herself on my leg.

The feeling of her gorgeous body surging and shivering against me blasts me out of my mind. I grab her ass in both hands and cram her down on my package.

She moans and sobs into my mouth without breaking away. She feels so captivatingly hot that I can't stop. I want to drive her to the stars right this minute even if she only gets off on my leg.

I pull her in deeper in a steady, unstoppable rhythm. Her body sways and undulates in my hands. She wants it. She's doing it. She's going to get off right here in front of me. Holy shit! How am I supposed to stand that?

One of my hands closes on her breast through her dress. Her body quakes at my touch. I dive under her dress and feel her bare thighs and hips bucking and grinding on my leg as she builds up speed and whines louder.

She whimpers in an agony of insatiable desire as her energy rises. I want to touch her, but I don't dare. I sneak my fingers into her panties, but I don't go any further than just holding onto her ass and pulling her into my rhythm.

She claws at my jacket, grips my shoulders, and struggles against the tempest raging inside her. Her features convulse all over the place. She keeps grimacing, moaning, and baring her teeth in animal madness. Christ, she's irresistible like this!

I force myself to settle down. She might let me go into her apartment with her and maybe even spend the night with her, but I don't want to. I don't want to rush her or anything between us.

She doesn't notice. She's too far gone already and she eventually works herself up to the peak of frenzy. She collapses on my shoulder sobbing and moaning in pathetic release. She sounds so impossibly sweet like this.

I straighten her dress, put my arms around her, and hold her while I kiss her hair and neck. I wait for her to power down and finally straighten up.

She raises her sex-drunk eyes to meet mine. That look makes me throb and ache for her. God, I want her so damn bad! I can't stand how beautiful and intoxicatingly appealing she is.

I stroke her hair and body, but I make sure to do it outside her dress. I don't touch her any more than that. I don't want to go any further with her—not tonight. We've covered enough ground tonight.

I eventually stand up straight. She holds onto me and huddles against me. I dig into her purse, find her keys, and then pick her up and carry her to her apartment.

I unlock the door, carry her inside, and into her bedroom. She has a nice, modern, upmarket apartment full of expensive, modern furniture. She must be doing well for herself.

I lay her down on her bed in her bedroom and put the keys on the pillow next to her. She rolls over, runs her fingers through her hair, and looks up at me with those eyes overflowing with so much meaning.

I have to kiss her. "You're beautiful," I whisper. "You're delicious and I want you more than anything."

Her lips pinch. She wants to ask me to stay, but she doesn't. She already understands why.

I lean all the way over and kiss her for a long time. "I'll call you this week about going out next Saturday," I murmur. "You stay sweet for me until then, okay?"

She nods. She looks like she's about to cry.

I can't stand that look of anguish and soul-crushing need in her eyes. I lean all the way over and put my arms around her. I hold her close for a minute. I don't know how to tell her what I'm feeling right now.

The fact that I feel this way about her absolutely requires that I leave. I want to stay more than anything and that's exactly why I have to leave. I have to.

I kiss her one more time and get out of there. My resolve will crumble if I stay here a second longer. Then I won't be able to leave at all and I'll wind up staying with her forever.

Chapter 20:
Nicole

I cruise around the internet on my computer at work when my phone buzzes on the desk next to me. I look down and see a text notification. It's from Rory. *Hey, gorgeous.*

I giggle and type back, *Hey, stud muffin.*

He sends back an emoji laughing with tears coming out of its eyes. *Can I take you out on Saturday night again? I have something special planned for you.*

I would love that. Do I need to wear any special protective clothing? Maybe something waterproof.

I laugh out loud. *What about a hazmat suit?*

That would be perfect. I'm sure you have one in your closet right now.

I can't stop grinning. *Eight o'clock again?*

Of course.

I can't wait. See you there.

He sends back a big throbbing heart emoji followed by a set of lipstick kisses. God dang, he is so sweet!

I loved kissing him and making out with him in the hallway, but it was the look in his eyes when he took me into my bedroom that really got me. I haven't been able to stop fantasizing about him since then.

I try to concentrate on work and get distracted by daydreaming about him. He really is unbelievably hot. He's a stud. He probably doesn't even realize how hot he is.

He knows about me now. That on its own excites me to distraction. I feel exposed and vulnerable to him. He knows more about me than any other man I've ever been with. He could reject me and break my heart in ways no one else ever has.

Feeling this vulnerable to someone turns me on beyond anything I've ever imagined possible. Just thinking about him feels like I might climax right here at my desk.

I somehow get through another hour of work and get ready to go out to lunch with my fellow reporters. We're doing a huge spread on a company setting up shop in Soho.

We'll be combining multiple stories, interviews, layout diagrams of their office complex, and a bunch of other interest pieces on their executive team and the company history.

I'm just picking up my phone and purse when I get a phone call. It's from my father. I don't want my co-workers to hear me speaking Italian, so I hustle outside and turn a corner behind the building before I answer.

I answer in English just because. "Hello?"

He answers in a defeated undertone. I always answer the phone in English even when I know it's him. He answers me in Italian. "It's over, Nicolina," he husks. "It's all over."

"What's over, Papa?" I ask in Italian. "What's wrong? You sound terrible."

"The building....the building is up for sale. The landlord canceled all the leases. I have to close the restaurant."

My world crumbles through my fingers at those words. "Oh, no."

"I tried a thousand ways to find out if the new owners will renew the leases. The landlord says he's canceling all the leases before he puts the building on the market. Whatever the new owner does is out of the landlord's hands. There's nothing I can do, bella. I have to close the restaurant. I have to pack up and....." His voice breaks with sobs. "I have nothing left without the restaurant. I don't know what will happen to me."

He breaks down sobbing on the other end of the line. I can't believe what I'm hearing. He didn't even cry when my mother died after they had been married for almost twenty years and had three children together. She left him to raise us alone and he never shed a single tear.

This will be the end of him. He's right about that. The restaurant is his life.

"I'm sorry, bella," he stammers. He keeps breaking down and letting out little whimpering moans. "I....I had to tell someone....You're the only one left."

"I'm on my way right now, Papa. I'm on my way. I'm coming to the restaurant right now. Stay there. I'm coming."

I hang up and hustle off in the other direction. To hell with lunch. To hell with the story. To hell with the *Record*. This is much more important.

I race down the stairs into the restaurant—and stop dead in my tracks the minute I walk into the dining room. The place doesn't sound right. Silence comes from the kitchen.

The sound of steam hissing, pans banging, and oil frying have always drifted out of the kitchen every other time I've come into this place. The lights are on, but the restaurant sounds way too quiet.

I used to hear my parents talking back there before my mother died. Later, I used to hear my father giving orders to my brothers while I worked out on the dining room floor.

Then there were all the times when I worked in the kitchen with him while my brothers worked the floor. I'll never hear those sounds again. It really is over.

Our family kept going as long as my father and I still lived here and he ran the restaurant. The restaurant kept the memories alive.

My brothers and I only had the courage to go out on our own and build lives for ourselves because we all knew the restaurant was still here the way we remembered it—or at least I felt that way. It was the anchor that kept the rest of us going.

Now that's gone. This is the end of our family—the only family I've ever known.

My father sits slumped in a chair at one of the tables. He's still wearing his apron. This is the first time I've ever seen him sit down in the dining room. He doesn't belong out here. He should be in the kitchen.

Silent tears streak down his cheeks. It's just the two of us now. We're the only two left at the end of the road.

We've been the only two left for a long time, but we both kept believing the dream—until now. Now it's over and we both stare into the abyss with nothing left to keep either of us going.

I don't know if I can survive losing the restaurant. I don't know how to think about my life or my future or my family or even myself without this.

How would I ever be able to explain anything to anyone without showing them this? No one would ever understand who I am. I wouldn't understand who I am.

Rory. Rory knows because he's seen it. He knows who I am and he loves and admires that about me. I don't know how I could ever get together with another man after this. It would have to be him. He's the only one left and he's the best of them anyway.

I stumble over to my father. I should touch him and comfort him, but I can't even do that. What am I supposed to say? Nothing will be okay after this. We're losing everything, including each other.

The restaurant bound us together as nothing ever could. I always knew where to find him. I always knew the world was still okay as long as he was still here running this place.

I always knew he would die someday. Then the restaurant would close and I would have to say goodbye to this part of my life.

I never thought it would die while he was still alive. I never let myself believe or even think he might lose the restaurant while he was still alive. I never planned for this and I'm certain he never did, either.

He has a retirement account. He'll be able to afford his living expenses without working around the clock to run this place.

He won't survive it, though. He won't live long without the restaurant. It's all he has. It's all he's ever wanted. It's his whole life, his family, his home.

He's more at home here than in the apartment where he was born and raised—where my brothers and I were born and raised.

I rest my hand on his shoulder and he completely breaks down crying. He covers his face with both hands. No one understands better than he does what's at stake here.

I don't even have the courage to ask what he needs to do to pack up the restaurant. I don't know what he'll do with the equipment or all the utensils or the old mops or all the extra food supplies he still has in the walk-in fridge.

I don't want to think about that. I should. I should help him plan. We need to talk about this, but I can't do that now. He's too devastated and so am I.

I pull up a chair in front of him and let him cry. I can't even talk to him and I don't ask him to talk to me. I'm the only one left. I'm all he has.

We sit in silence for two hours before I tell him to stand up. I take him back to our apartment and sit him in a chair at the kitchen table. This is the first time any of us have sat at this table since I was a kid.

My mom used to feed me and my brothers dinner here in the evenings while she was still alive. Then all four of us would go down to the restaurant to help my father with the dinner rush.

Later, after my mom died, my brothers and I would come home from school and have dinner alone. My brothers would prepare leftover food that my father put in the fridge for us.

They would heat up the food and the three of us would eat and do our homework before going down to the restaurant for the evening. I can't remember a single night of my childhood that didn't pass the same way.

I park my father at the table, go back to the restaurant, and get some of the leftovers from yesterday out of the walk-in. Why waste the food if he has to get rid of it anyway?

I take it back to the apartment and heat it up for both of us. He starts crying again when I put the food in front of him.

I sit across from him at the table. I don't have to do anything. I just have to be here with him. I have to be the one person in the world that he shares this with. This is both of us. We're both dying here.

I eat my food while I wait for him to pull himself together. He eventually pulls an old cotton handkerchief out of his pocket, blows his nose on it, wipes his face, and starts eating.

"I don't know what I'm going to do," he croaks between mouthfuls.

"I'm sure you can sell the equipment to a wholesaler," I tell him. "They can come and pick up everything in one of their moving vans. Then you don't have to worry about finding buyers for each and every piece. Sometimes restaurant supply companies will buy everything in the place as one lot. You won't have to figure out what to do with everything."

He nods down at his plate. "That's a good idea, Nicolina."

"You and I can divide up the extra food. There's no need to waste it when you've already paid for it."

Tears start to flow down his cheeks while we talk. "I can't afford to move the restaurant anywhere else," he quavers. "I would have to lay out for marketing and promotion to let everyone know where I was moving—and I wouldn't be able to afford the lease on another place. I can only afford it because it's in that basement."

I nod. That's what I suspected. The rent on the basement is controlled by the city. The landlord can't raise it more than a certain amount relative to inflation. My father would never have been able to afford to stay in business for so long otherwise.

"Do you want me to call around and find a broker to buy everything in one load?" I ask. "Then you don't have to do it."

He nods at nothing. "Thank you, bella."

I feel myself getting choked up. "We should find something for you to do so you aren't sitting here alone all day afterward. You should go teach cooking classes somewhere."

"How would I do that?" he whimpers. "My English is no good."

"Your English is just fine. You speak English perfectly well when you have to. Why do you sell yourself short? Anything would be better than you sitting here feeling hopeless and useless all the time. You have to do something and you're so good at cooking."

I get a brief flash of my conversation with Vivian Salazar. I want to tell my father to start a YouTube channel and content creation business teaching people how to make Italian food.

That would be the perfect job for him. He could share his passion and expertise with the world. Now I understand why Derek encouraged Vivian to do it. What an act of love that was.

I don't say that. Maybe I'll say it later, but not now. My father is too upset about all of this. It's all too raw.

Chapter 21: Rory

I show up to Nicole's apartment at eight o'clock sharp as usual. I can't wait to take her to my surprise date. She'll love it—or she better love it.

She opens the door and makes the most half-hearted attempt to smile at me. "Hi," she breathes.

"Hi." I lean in and kiss her on the cheek. She doesn't respond at all.

I take her hand and lead her toward the elevator. She doesn't look at me. She barely seems aware of me. Something must be wrong.

Did something happen in the last couple of days? Maybe she changed her mind about us. Maybe I'm too messed up for her. Maybe she wants someone with as clear a sense of family as she has. I wouldn't blame her if that's the reason.

She doesn't tell me not to take her out, so we ride down the elevator in silence and I put her in my car. "How was your week?" I ask to break the ice.

She shrugs. "It was pretty good. We're doing a big story about that new Proton Limited development downtown. We're partnering with the *Connection* with two dozen reporters all collaborating on one story with multiple articles. So that's been keeping everyone busy."

Her voice sounds flat. Her heart isn't in it when she says her week is going good. It sounds like the opposite.

"Oh, and Wayne Grodin is getting ready to retire," she adds as an afterthought. "He's been with the *Record* for fifteen years, so the whole place is in a tizzy trying to figure out who's going to replace him."

"Does Capitol Media have someone picked out yet?"

"They have to advertise the job on the open market. They aren't allowed to mention if they already have someone picked out. They have to take applicants from anywhere to make sure they get the most qualified candidate instead of just giving it to whoever happens to be kissing their ass this week."

"Have you thought about applying for the position?" I ask. "You would be great at that. The *Record* needs someone like you."

She turns away from me to look out the window. "Naw. I don't think so."

"Why not?" I take her hand and lace my fingers into hers. She feels dead. "What's on your mind? Is that what's bothering you? It can't be if you said you had a good week."

She doesn't answer. I drive north to the far end of Manhattan, pull into a park, and follow a bunch of winding driveways until I angle my car in front of the Cloisters Museum in Fort Tryon Park.

She smiles for the first time when she looks out the window. "What are we doing here?"

"I told you I was planning to take you somewhere special. Come on. Get out."

I open her door for her. She beams and her eyes sparkle the way they should.

She lowers her voice to a whisper when I start to unlock the entrance doors. "How did you get into this place when the museum is closed?"

"I still have a few tricks up my sleeve."

"You aren't breaking in illegally, are you?"

"Of course not. I wouldn't want the burglar alarm and the Police to interrupt our date."

She giggles. I take her hand, lead her inside, and lock the door behind us. I have to turn on a flashlight to lead her through a bunch of corridors to the central courtyard in the middle of the four cloisters.

I escort her to a candlelit table in the middle of the courtyard. We're the only people here. I have all the food laid out in warming pans on a separate table.

I seat her at the table and start serving her. She smiles at me, but she gets serious again when I sit down in front of her and we start eating.

She pokes the food with her fork, but she doesn't seem too interested to find out if it's still alive. She doesn't look up at me or ask me how I did this when I've already told her I don't cook. She's a million miles away.

I don't know how to get through to her, but I can't sit here wondering if she's planning to end things between us.

"Are you upset or unhappy about something between us?" I ask. "Is that why you're so distant?"

"I'm really sorry!" She throws down her fork too fast and it clangs on the side of the plate. "I shouldn't have come out with you tonight. This was a really bad idea."

"Are you saying going out with me at all is a bad idea? You don't have to go out with me at all, you know. Just tell me if you don't want to go out."

"It isn't you—not at all. Please don't think that. I'm just really preoccupied right now. The building whose basement my father leases for the restaurant—the building went up for sale this week and the landlord canceled all the leases. My father has to close the restaurant and we've been scrambling this whole week to figure out how to sell his equipment and what to do with all the other stuff. He's a mess. I don't even know how he's gonna survive this. He's not handling it well at all, so I have to be the one to call around and find a broker to buy up all the equipment and plates and supplies and stuff. I try to encourage him to start teaching cooking or something to move into the next phase of his life, but he's so broken up about it that he doesn't even hear me. He keeps breaking down crying all the time and isn't able to handle anything and that leaves me with no one to talk to about how I feel about the whole thing....."

Her voice cracks with buried tears, and without warning, she breaks down in front of me crying into her hands. I can't say a word. I can only sit here and listen.

This is a disaster. The restaurant means everything—to both of them. It's their whole history and family together. I'm not surprised Vitale is crumbling without it—and she's right. Him crumbling leaves her with nowhere to turn and no one to talk to.

She probably hasn't talked to anyone about how she feels. I'm the only one because I'm the only other person in her life who even knows about the restaurant.

She tears her hands off her face, grabs the folded cloth napkin next to her plate, and scrapes it across her cheeks. "I'm really sorry, Rory," she chokes. "This is a really romantic date and I can see that you put a lot of effort into this, but I really think you better just take me home. I can't deal with this right now and I feel too guilty that I can't give you the attention you deserve."

I don't need her attention right now, but I really don't feel like eating anything, either—not now.

I put my fork down. "Okay, sweetheart. Let's go."

I stand up and take her hand. She really starts crying on our way back to the car. I don't want her to feel guilty about this. She has more important things on her mind—like how to get through the next however long it will take for her father to pull his life together.

She sobs all the way back to her building and all the way back upstairs to her apartment. I stop her outside and pull her into my arms. I don't even try to kiss her. I just hold her while she cries.

She's still fighting down anguish and failing to control her features when I push her back and hold her at arm's length. "I'll call you this week to check on you, okay?" I tell her.

She clamps her lips shut and nods. God, she's so miserable! I kiss her on the forehead and say, "Good night." She's too upset even to answer me. She unlocks the door and goes inside alone.

I don't know what's going to happen to her, but she has to work it out before she can continue anything with me.

Chapter 22: Nicole

I wake up numb and bruised on Sunday morning. I feel terrible about the way I ended my date with Rory last night, but I wasn't good company for him—not with this disaster hanging over my head.

Now I have to face the nightmare of going to the restaurant and helping my father pack up the few possessions he plans to keep before the brokers come and take everything else away. I don't look forward to this.

I sit up and put my feet on the floor. It takes me a long time to summon the energy to get to my feet. I didn't even change out of my clothes last night. I slept in my clothes.

Crying in front of Rory let the genie out of the bottle. Now I can't put these wretched feelings back in the hole where I've been hiding them all this time. I finally feel just what a colossal disaster this is—for me as much as for my father.

Tears spring to my eyes as soon as I sit up and I start bawling my eyes out again. I have to get it all out now. I can't let my father see me like this. I need to be there for him and help him get out of the restaurant once and for all.

I cry as much for Rory as I do for myself, my father, my family, or the restaurant. I can't even accept the care and attention of a good man as long as I have this hanging over my head.

He didn't even ask me to try to finish our date. He just understood and ended it. I hate to think of the effort and planning he put into that dinner at the Cloisters. He probably paid someone a lot of money to be able to use the courtyard for the night.

That is such a romantic gesture and I couldn't even enjoy it. I let him down, but he doesn't care. He only cares about doing what's best for me in the moment. He didn't ask for anything except to give me whatever it is that I need at the time.

I want him in my life. I just don't know how to with all this other stuff going on. How long will I get caught up with taking care of my father? How long do I have to put my life on hold? What if I miss out on any chance between me and Rory because of this?

He might be willing to wait, but I'm not. He's the best man I've ever met and he obviously wants to be with me.

I wouldn't feel right about being happy with him as long as my father is in such bad shape. I wouldn't even feel right about telling my father that I finally found the man I want to spend my life with.

That's what this is. He's the one. He's the only one—and not because he's the only one who knows about the restaurant. He's the only one who knows about everything. He knows about the club. He knows about the hotel. He knows about all of it.

He's the safe deposit box of all my most dangerous secrets. I trust him with all of the most explosive parts of myself—the parts someone would really be able to use to hurt me. I trust him with it because he already knows and I'm already safe with him.

I heave myself off the bed, take a shower, and change into jeans and a work shirt before I drag myself out of the apartment. I don't want to. I don't want to face today or the rest of this year or even the rest of this decade.

Do I really have to spend the next twenty years of my life watching my father fall apart in front of my eyes—or even the next year—or however long it takes him to completely check out and leave this world behind?

I don't want to do that, but I can't give him a reason to live. He has to find that for himself.

I take my packing tape dispenser and my work gloves, drag my heels down the basement stairs probably for the last time, and walk into the restaurant.

I stop dead in my tracks again when I smell the aroma of food coming out of the kitchen. All the usual sounds of sizzling, banging, bubbling, and rummaging drift through service window—and then I hear my father singing.

He hasn't sung in decades—not since before my mom died. His deep, resonant voice echoes off the walls and fills the whole place with vibrations. That sound sends a shiver up my spine.

He hasn't laid out any boxes. All the tables and chairs stand in their usual places with fresh new tablecloths and folded napkins in their proper places. It's still mid-morning, so he hasn't lit the candles for dinner yet.

I stare around me in shock. I don't even get a chance to move before my father happens to pass the service window and sees me standing there.

"Bella!" He rushes me, kisses me on the cheek, and hugs me. I can't even raise my arms to hug him back. "It's a beautiful day! I love today! Tonight is going to be so nice! You should stay for dinner. I'm making braciola. You always liked that...."

"What are you doing, Papa?!" I blurt out. "We're supposed to be packing up! Remember? We have to get ready for the brokers to come and take all of this away."

"Not anymore!" He cups both my cheeks and kisses me on the nose. "A miracle happened. Someone else bought the building and renewed all the leases. I'm back in business! Now come on. I need you to help m e...."

He turns back toward the kitchen. I dive for him and grab his arm. "Wait a minute, Papa. Who bought the building? Who pulled off the miracle?"

"I don't know. Some company with a name a mile long." He waves that away. "It's not a person. It's some conglomerate or something or other. I don't know the details. The landlord called me this morning to tell me. That's all I know. Now come on. Enough talk. Food is much more important."

He walks away laughing. I get a sinking feeling about this. I better not find out what I think I'm about to find out.

I rush after him and grab him again. "Where's the lease paperwork, Papa? You must have signed a new lease with this conglomerate. Where's the paperwork? Show it to me."

He frowns at me. "What's wrong with you? This is a dream come true. Why are you so bent out of shape about it?"

"Just show me the paperwork." I have to stop myself from shrieking at him. He has no idea. "Just show me. I need to see it."

"It's exactly the same lease—the same rent and terms and everything." He heads for his tiny office in the back of the restaurant. We have to dodge a bunch of stacks of supply boxes on the way. He clicks around on his computer and points at a PDF in his email. "See? Everything is the same."

I bend over to read the document. The new owner of this building is a corporation named Mercury Holdings. That tells me nothing. I grab my phone and do a quick search on them.

It comes up with a website that lists the company as a REIT—a real estate investment trust. They go around buying real estate investments that return a share of the profit to their shareholders as an investment dividend.

I navigate around until I finally find the shareholder information on their trustee board and governing body. Rory Kahn is listed as the founder and Chairman of the Board of Trustees. I knew it.

"I have to go, Papa." I kiss him on the cheek. "Enjoy yourself tonight. I'll talk to you later."

"Oh, I will definitely enjoy myself tonight. Hey!" He spins around when he sees me rushing out of the room. "Where are you going?"

"I have to do something! It's important."

I rush upstairs, down the street, and hop the nearest subway. I don't even know what I'm going to say to Rory about this. I don't even know what to think about this.

Why did I think he would let this fly? He wouldn't leave my family high and dry—especially not when he saw how upset I was about it.

What can I possibly say to him—thank you? That's ridiculous.

I ride the subway to the neighborhood nearest his apartment. I don't even know if he's home. He could be anywhere. It's nine o'clock on a Sunday morning. He could be sound asleep for all I know.

Chapter 23:
Nicole

I feel my hands shaking by the time I ride the elevator to Rory's floor and approach his apartment door. What am I even doing here? How do I even talk to him about this? What does it even mean that he bought my father's building—or arranged for the trust to buy it?

I ring the doorbell. Maybe Rory won't even be home. Maybe he'll be working today. I wouldn't be surprised.

I'm just about to chicken out and run for it when the door rips open too fast. He obviously wasn't expecting me to show up—and I wasn't expecting me to show up.

He answers wearing a pair of dark blue sweatpants and nothing else. He's covered in sweat and his sweat-soaked hair hangs in his eyes. He must have been working out just now.

He carries a towel in one hand and he's in the act of wiping the sweat off his face when he answers the door.

He freezes when he sees me standing there. I freeze, too. This is the first time I've seen him with his shirt off—or in anything other than a perfectly appointed suit.

His eyes go hard like I did something wrong by coming to his apartment. "Are you okay?" he asks.

"You......you bought my father's building.....didn't you?"

He finishes wiping his face and then rubs the towel over the back of his neck. "I didn't, but I arranged for one of my companies to do it—yeah. Is that a problem?"

I hurl myself at him, throw my arms around him, and kiss him. I don't know what else to do or say. Nothing else seems to fit what he's just done for my family.

He stumbles under my weight and then attacks me back just as hard. I don't even care that I'm getting his sweat all over my clothes. I want to.

He grabs me, pulls me into the apartment, and throws the door shut behind me. He lets go of his towel and it falls on the floor. He tries to turn me toward the apartment. I don't even get a look at it. We're both attacking each other too fast.

I try to touch him all over. His body skyrockets me into a frenzy. He's beyond hot, ripped, and his shoulders are much broader than his suits do him justice.

His beefy arms get in the way of me doing anything. I just have to hold on while he claws at my clothes trying to tear them off me fast enough. He tries to turn me around and we both stumble into the wall by the door. His weight falls on top of me.

All the furious desire from our last make-out session erupts back to life. He grabs my breasts much harder through my clothes and squeezes hard enough to make me whine with aching desire.

Burning heat sears between my legs. I want him. I want all of him. I want the man who keeps coming through for me every time I need him to. He has to come through for me now and I know he wants to.

He doesn't pull away this time. He pulverizes me under his weight, sticks his knee between my legs, and grinds his hardness down on me so I feel how much he's throbbing for it. When was the last time he really let himself let go?

I want now to be the time. I want to be the one he lets go with. I want to feel him let go with me the way he let me let go with him last time.

I arch my hips into those brutal thrusts. He digs his package between my legs and makes me scream as a blast of desire splits me apart. I need him to conquer me. I need to go all the way with him. I don't want to wait anymore.

He comes at me just as hard, picks up one of my legs, and works his hips between my thighs so he can pump up into me from the right angle. We both still have all our clothes on—except that he's shirtless.

I never imagined he could be so hot. His muscles bulge every time he grabs me. He covers my face with kisses and gnaws down my neck getting closer to my shirt collar.

I cry out in shivering excitement, and lightning quick, he tears his hand down my shirt and rips it open so he can burrow lower into me.

He can't grind on me and taste my body at the same time. He scoops up both my legs, lifts me all the way up to his waist, and uses his weight to hold me against the wall so he can attack my chest.

I scream again and try to grab his shoulders, his head—any part of him I can get.

He seizes my wrists and pins them to the wall while he rips my bra aside with his teeth. There's no stopping him. I shriek as his hot, torturous mouth closes on my breasts one after the other. He dives back and forth between them mauling, biting, sucking, and teasing.

I thrash against his hold as mind-blowing excitement takes me over. This is it. This is the moment when I finally give myself to him for good. I need this so bad. I need him. I need everything he is, including his ferocity right now.

He doesn't let go of my breasts when he releases my wrists and scoops his powerful arms under my seat to support my weight. He cradles me in his arms with my legs still wrapped around his waist while he carries me away from the wall.

I'm too out of my mind from the sensation of his mouth on my nipples. I lose track of where he's taking me until he steps down a few stairs into a sunken living room.

A circular couch surrounds a circular coffee table in front of big bay windows looking out at Central Park across the street. This is a big, luxurious apartment, but not as big as some I've seen. It still has an intimate, lived-in feel.

He goes down on his knees next to the couch and sets me down to sit on it even as he keeps his arms around me. He breaks away from my breasts, straightens up, and kisses me with those sharp eyes of his shining right in front of me.

He slows down to his former crawl. He kisses slowly, carefully, all the while exploring me with his eyes like he just can't quite bring himself to believe that I want him this much.

He raises his hands ever so slowly.....and deliberately pulls my shirt off my shoulders. He holds my eyes in an unbreakable hold while he unclips my bra behind my back and slides the straps off.

My skin tingles. He makes me tremble at every touch.

His warm hands glide up my back to my neck, down to my waist, and back up to my bare breasts. His fingers close around both my breasts to knead, twist, pinch, and play with them to make me moan into his mouth.

My eyes slip out of focus. He's going to do it with me. Every inch of his rock-hard body tells me that. He doesn't plan to hold back this time. I'm here in his apartment. He's undressing me on his couch. He wants me and I want him.

He breaks my soul open with his hands touching me all over. I want him more than anything.

I hold his gaze just as straight when I lower my hand to his waistband and dive inside. He's wearing a pair of stretchy cotton boxers underneath and his hard shaft strains to get out.

He falls into my hand and his eyes turn to granite when I start touching him back. He doesn't change his pace or the pressure on my breasts. He keeps playing with them and flooding me with more excruciating passion than I can stand.

I moan in aching desire when I feel how hard he is. I want to steer him into me, but I can't even concentrate when he's touching me like this.

His lips keep swirling in mine. His tongue coils around mine to rush waves of heat down my body to my swollen flesh between my legs. I need him. I need him to take me right this minute.

He reads my mind and slides his hands down to my pants. He doesn't take his eyes off me when he unbuttons them and scoots them down to sit me on the couch completely naked.

I don't even notice that. His eyes hold me captive. I can't get away. I don't want to get away. I want to vanish into those eyes and all the overpowering sensations he's giving me.

He pushes his sweats and shorts down with one hand and pulls me by my hips to the edge of the couch. His eyes command me to give myself to him the way I need to. He doesn't do it for me. He waits for me to steer his prick into the right position.

He doesn't lean in and take me. He pulls me one brutal inch after another until he works me down on his shaft. Only then does he start stroking into me—slowly, deliberately, under masterful control.

He keeps hold of my eyes at all times even when his hands start making their inevitable migration all over my body. He grabs my thighs to push them farther apart. He crushes my breasts harder and twists my nipples until I whimper and scream in ecstasy.

His shaft breaks me in half with more pleasure than I can handle. I try to rear back on the couch to arch into him, but he won't release me.

He straps his arms even tighter behind my back and lifts me into his thrusts. His lips, tongue, and eyes force me to stay locked onto him no matter what. I have to keep looking into his eyes even as he conquers my deepest being.

His fingers crawl down my spine to grip my ass—and then he sneaks around the thickness of his shaft to tease my clitoris while he penetrates me.

I explode in a dizzy, screaming orgasm from that extra stimulation. I fall apart and collapse into his arms, but he isn't finished—not by a million miles. I came here to give myself to him. Now I'm his for the taking.

He tightens his grip, crushes me in his muscular arms, and picks me up off the couch so I'm not even supporting my own weight anymore. I couldn't support myself if I tried.

He hauls me into himself at his own rhythm. He slams me down on his tool with breaking power. Every stroke fires me into the stratosphere on a rising tide of escalating climax.

I scream and convulse in his arms too much to kiss him anymore. He tries, and when that fails, he crams his forehead against mine gasping, panting, and rasping at me through bared, snarling teeth. His features transform into a mask of pure animal madness.

He doesn't let up even for a second. My thrashing, tortured contortions and wailing screams only encourage him. He thumps me down on his straining meat to split me in half. I can't take this, but I can't stop, either.

His husky snarls come out in choked, broken roars as he builds up power. He controls all my movements so I can't get away. I need him to take control right now while I fly completely apart at the seams.

He escalates as each layer of my defenses crumbles before him. He consumes every shred of fevered passion I unleash on him. Nothing stops him or makes him hesitate even once.

His hands cover my whole body. He teases me to insanity in every possible way even as he maintains the same rising beat.

My gushing wetness drips down his shaft and coats my ass. Everything he does makes me feel insatiably sexy and irresistible to his most carnal desires.

He blasts me apart into one reeling explosion after another. I fall back into his arms even as I fight to contain all this power erupting from me at once.

The sensation of his length exciting me from the inside sends me spiraling off the deep end of consciousness into outer space. I can't fight him. I don't want to fight him, but my body tosses and struggles just from the colossal impact of his body stroking into mine.

I'm so far gone that I don't even know what's happening by the time he swivels me sideways, lays me down longways on the couch, and climbs on top of me.

He lowers his weight on me with his hips still corkscrewing between my legs. The sensation changes to such a delicious tide of bliss that I can't stand it.

He starts kissing me again and our eyes sink shut on both sides into a dark, warm, ocean of succulent, dreamy rapture. Our bodies move in a steady beat of our hearts combining into one.

I wrap myself around him and circle my tongue in his mouth even as his explores the depths of my being. I hug him down on top of me and feel his heart pounding right against mine.

His arms clamp around me even tighter as he picks up the pace. He brings me back to the same brink of detonation without me even realizing it.

He untangles his arms from around me, pushes himself up, and shifts one leg up past my hip so he can drill into me from a different angle. His features turn to solid, furious stone as he launches into a powerful, driving, jackhammer rhythm.

His hard, unwavering eyes stare straight down into my soul gone completely out of this world on so much earth-shattering rapture. I can't think except that he possesses me in every dimension now.

He already held my heart by the strings. He owns all my secrets and still protects me. He'll protect this, too. It isn't possible for him to see me like this without realizing how fully he possesses me.

He holds me in that nether zone of near-total annihilation while he takes me the rest of the way out of this world into chaos and disintegration. I can only go there because he's the one doing this.

He's the one holding me in the palm of his hand. I can go all the way out into space because he's the one who will bring me back when this is all over.

Chapter 24: Rory

I let my mouth sink onto that soft place between Nicole's neck and her shoulder. A delicate shudder passes down her body when I close my mouth and teeth in a soft, wet, succulent bite on that fragile skin.

Her body trembles in my arms. She tries to struggle, but not against my hold. Her body reacts to my touch. She can't decide whether to fight to get away from the intensity of that sensation or to throw herself back against me again.

Her naked ass, back, and thighs lie against me in the darkness of my bedroom. Her hair spills over my face when she moves her head.

Every taste of her flesh leaves me breathless and ravenous for more. I just spent all night taking her again and again. She never stops me. She gives herself to me fully every time even when she's so exhausted from climaxing so much.

I could take her for the next week and never get tired. Doing it with her gives me superhuman strength. It affects my nervous system like some kind of drug. I can't sleep when she's around. I can't think about anything but attacking her and conquering her all over again.

I should let her sleep, but it's already four in the morning. "You have to work today, don't you?" I whisper in her ear.

"Yes, and so do you," she murmurs in the darkness. "We have to get up soon."

"Not yet," I breathe and pull her tighter against me. The thought of her leaving makes me animalistically, irrationally possessive of her. I don't want her out there in the world. I want to keep her in my bed forever.

"What's going to happen now?" Her voice strains.

"I want you," I murmur. "I want you always. I want more of this. I want you to come back here after work tonight. That's what I want." I press my mouth against her ear. I want to whisper straight into her mind and soul. "Say that's what you want, too."

She trembles in my arms and her skin electrifies with magical energy. She's getting turned on by my voice. "Yes," she whispers. "I want that, too."

"I'll take you out to dinner tomorrow. I need to make up for last time. We can decide after dinner if you want to come back here."

"I will come back here afterward." She tries to turn her head, but she can't quite make it. "Did you think I didn't? Do you think I don't want more of it, too?"

"Just go out with me first. We can talk about all of that later."

I let my mouth crawl around the back of her neck to the soft, sensitive spot right at the base of her hairline. Every particle of her—every cell and throbbing blood vessel—they all hum with so much preciousness that I can't even stand it.

Lying next to her drives me out of my mind—and yet I can't even do it with her anymore. I'm in love. This is what it feels like. I'm so turned on by her and so over the moon over her that I can't even move. Just holding her in my arms feels like a cataclysm.

She spasms when I kiss the back of her neck. She mews in a low, agonized whine of pure, tortured arousal. Everything I do seems to have the same effect on her that she has on me.

I only have to breathe on her or look deep into her eyes or drag my lips across her skin. She collapses in this pathetic, whimpering, helpless turmoil of rapture whether we do it or not.

Everything I've ever heard or learned says it shouldn't be this way. Everything I've ever heard or learned says she should need to warm up before she gets to that point.

Kissing her, breathing on her, looking into her eyes, and dragging my lips across her skin are supposed to be the warm-up—the early-stage warm-up. They're supposed to be almost casual. They aren't supposed to buckle her in whimpering orgasm just from that.

I could almost believe she was faking it except that it keeps happening exactly the same way again and again. She doesn't just do it once to get it over with and tell me we're done. She keeps coming at me and building up at the slightest touch.

Is she in love with me as deeply as I am with her? She sure acts like it. She doesn't get up to leave. She doesn't try to get away from me. She acts and talks like she never wants to leave.

That's the way I feel, but I suppose we ought to be reasonable about this. I don't want to tell her I want to keep her chained to my bed around the clock and never let another man lay eyes on her. I'm guessing that wouldn't go down well even though I do want that.

She writhes again at the sensation of my lips inching down her spine toward her back. Her skin is far more sensitive than any other woman I've ever been with. She responds off the charts to any stimulation, even just looking at her.

I could roll her onto her back and let my gaze travel all over her milky white breasts and thighs. She would undulate in front of me and get turned on by my gaze. It happened more than once last night.

I don't want to loosen my arms from around her. I want to feel her right here against my heart. I want to feel that I'm holding her and she's mine—for now, at least.

Her ass touches my prick when she arches like that. She contorts in my arms like she's having another orgasm right now. She turns me on so much that I start to get hard even though I know I shouldn't.

She works her ass backward onto my knob until I can't help but glide into her moist, soft, juicy flesh. She moans high and broken when her muscles clamp around me.

My body takes over and I stroke into her while she thrashes in my arms. She seems to like it better when I hold her tighter. Maybe she feels safer to really let go when she feels me taking control of her.

I flex my midsection to drive her down on me. She screams and all that energy erupts out of her beyond all proportion. She unleashes like nothing I've ever seen or even heard of. She roars out in an agony of release that goes on and on as long as I keep taking her.

I can't last as long as I should—not when she acts like this. She eventually milks the next excruciating jet of fire from my insides. She keeps draining me again and again without end. How long can this go on before one of us taps out?

I collapse once I unload into her. She wilts in my arms still spasming and whining in what sounds like pain. I know better now. She has trouble tolerating the catastrophic energy surges taking her over each time. They shatter her senses, but she can't stop them.

I want to kiss her some more. I want to taste the delicious smell and sensation of her skin in my mouth, but that would only drive her crazy.

I settle for burying my face in her hair and inhaling her scent. I don't want to lose this. She's delectable. She's exquisite—and she's mine. I know that now. She might not know it yet, but I do.

I drift off for an hour before she stirs in my arms. "One of us should get up," she murmurs.

"You first," I mutter into her hair.

She giggles. "You would have to loosen your arms for me to do that."

"Forget it," I growl. "You'll have to find another way."

"I love it when you go all caveman on me." She wriggles in my arms to turn around and face me. She kisses me all over my face to wake me up. She even kisses my eyes and down my temples to my ears and neck.

Her lips light me up and a rush of heat shoots to my crotch again. "Do you really like it?" I ask. "That isn't what I was taught by women in the know."

She giggles and her hand closes around my shaft. "Do you think I could say no to this?"

"What are you going to do with it—now that you got it?"

"Oh, I'm sure I could come up with something to do with it. It seems like it wants to do something, doesn't it?"

I should look away, but I can't take my eyes off her. She rolls on top of me, steers me inside herself, and sits up to ride me like that.

She keeps smiling at me even as the color flushes her cheeks and her lips shiver with the energy building up inside her. I grab her hips and bump up into her from below to make her gasp and then scream.

I need more of her. She says she wants me to go caveman her. I sit up to put my arms around her, but she jumps off and shrieks with laughter before I get there.

"You are gonna pay for that!" I yell after her as she disappears into the bathroom.

She won't stop laughing, not even when she switches on the shower. I sink back into bed still raging hard. I have half a mind to go into the shower with her and go all caveman on her there. I'll show her what going caveman on her really looks like.

I have to smile at her antics, though. She really knows how to wind me up.

I settle down while I wait for her to get out of the shower. She showed up wearing work clothes yesterday, so she'll have to go home and change before work.

She comes out of the bathroom looking all gorgeous with a white towel wrapped around her body and another one twisted around her hair. She grins when she sees me lying in bed with the sheet across my lower half and my arm behind my head.

"Do you want me to make you breakfast?" she asks.

"You're the only person qualified to do any cooking around here, so if you want to cook me breakfast, I'll be your humble servant for life."

She laughs and blushes. "Something tells me you would never be anyone's humble servant even for a few minutes. I don't suppose you have a blow-dryer here, do you?"

"No, and I don't have any eyelash curlers or tampons or mascara, either. Sorry, baby. You'll have to get your own."

She laughs again. "Darn. I thought I could count on you to have my back."

"I'm not the one who told you to come over here yesterday and throw yourself at me. You should have come prepared."

She shoots me a smirk over her shoulder. "You didn't seem too offended at the time."

"Offended? I was absolutely horrified. I was in fear for my life. That's the only reason I went along with it."

She bursts out laughing. "I have to go out to the living room to get dressed. Why don't you take a shower, get dressed, and try to get over the trauma while I make breakfast?"

Chapter 25: Rory

Nicole leaves the bedroom and I somehow find the willpower to get out of bed. The thought of her cooking me breakfast eventually becomes too tempting to resist. I take a shower, put on my suit for the day, and do my hair before I go out to the living room.

She's just putting the food on the plates. She's made some kind of open-faced sandwiches with eggs, cheese, and veggies I usually use for salads.

She's sautéed them with tons of spices and somehow whipped up some delicious sauce that swims over the bread and puddles on the plate. She sits down on the stool next to me at the counter and picks up her knife and fork to cut up the sandwiches like a pro.

I copy the way she eats since I obviously have no flippin' clue what I'm doing here. "You can come over and cook for me all the time," I tell her.

She giggles and then looks up at me. "Can I ask you something?"

"Sure. Anything."

"I mean, it's really more that I want to tell you something. You won't get offended or anything like that, will you—because I don't want to bother you with it if you are."

"Just tell me what it is. I don't have to sign an indemnity agreement for you to ask me questions. It isn't like you don't already know the worst about me."

"Not quite," she mutters under her breath.

I look up to frown at her. "What's wrong? Now I'm worried."

"I mean.....earlier....when you said....."

I wait for her to get whatever it is off her chest.

She flounders for a minute and then blurts out, "You said you were terrified and in fear of your life. You said that's the only reason you went along with it. I wouldn't want to....you know....bring up anything...from your past....."

I look away. "You didn't—and you won't."

"I don't want to pry or anything.....but how would I know? I mean, how would I know if I was doing something that hurt you...or scared you....or reminded you of something you didn't want to be reminded of?"

I put another bite of the food in my mouth while I think about how to answer her. I feel sick to my stomach right now, but I don't want to insult her by not eating the food she worked hard to make for me.

I realize I'm taking too long to answer. Now she's getting worried. She stands up, takes her half-eaten breakfast to the kitchen, and practically throws the plate into the sink with all the food still on it.

"Just forget I asked, okay?" Her voice shakes. "I just want to take as good care of you as you've always taken care of me. That's the only reason I asked. Just pretend the last ten minutes never happened, okay?"

She sounds like she's about to burst into tears. She's just winding up to get really upset about this.

I put my fork down too fast. "Nicole—look at me."

She stops on the other side of the counter, glances at me, and turns away biting her lips. "I'm sorry, Rory!" she croaks.

"Baby....you won't scare me or hurt me or remind me of anything. I promise you that."

"But....how do you know? It could happen."

"It won't happen....because all the people who did anything to me were men. You have nothing to worry about."

Her features spasm and she nods down at her plate in the sink. How did this conversation go so wrong?

"Bring your breakfast over here and sit next to me," I tell her. "You need to eat before you go to work and you are NOT wasting this food—not after you worked so hard to make it for me. Come on, baby. Come sit by me. You can ask me anything you want—even that."

She picks up her plate and slumps onto the stool next to me. She has never looked more miserable.

"Would you like me to tell you what happened?" I ask. "Would it make you feel better if you knew everything?"

"No!" she exclaims too loudly and immediately corrects herself. "I don't need to know all that. I just...." She spins around to confront me. "Why didn't you tell anyone? Why did you let them get away with it for so long? They drew a stipend from Social Services for ten whole years—a stipend they were supposed to spend on food and clothes and medical care for you—while you were living on the street. How could you let them get away with that?" She looks away. "I shouldn't even be asking you this. It's none of my business."

"Everything about me is your business, sweetheart. You have every right to know everything about me—the good, the bad, and the ugly. You would have to know all of that so you could decide if you even want to get involved with me." Now it's my turn to look away. "You might decide I'm too fucked up for you to have anything to do with."

"No, I won't! How can you even say that? You're one of the strongest, nicest, most put-together people I've ever met! You've always been there for me. You aren't damaged or fucked up or anything! Why would you even say something like that about yourself?"

I shrug. "They never got away with anything. Believe me."

"How do you know?"

"Because they got busted—big time. They might have thought at the time that they were getting away with something, but they didn't. It came back to bite them in the ass and now they're doing time up in Rikers where they belong."

She blinks at me from the side. "Are you sure?"

"Of course. I testified against them."

She gasps out loud. "Really?! What happened?"

"It was after I started to get really successful. I gave my first interview where the reporter asked about my background and the whole story came out. Someone from CPS contacted me about a week later. He had tracked down the family I ran away from. The service was planning on taking them to court for Social Services fraud for taking all that money. They asked me to testify about when, where, and for how long I lived outside of the house without the family reporting it. Then CPS found some of my medical records and the whole thing went down the pipe from there."

Her jaw drops. "What did they find?"

I can't look at her, but I have to tell her. I owe her that minimum of an explanation. "About a week after I ran away from the house, I collapsed in an alley where I was living. It was the alley behind a certain restaurant where I used to scavenge food out of the dumpster. The owner knew I was there and called CPS on me a few times, but I saw them coming and I hid from them so they wouldn't send me back to the house. Anyway, about a week after I started staying in this alley, I collapsed back there and one of the dishwashers found me and called the paramedics. They took me to the hospital where the doctors found certain injuries on me and......." I take a deep breath, but I can't keep my voice steady. I've never told anyone this. "I had hepatitis—sexually transmitted hepatitis. I also had bruising and tearing around my mouth and anus from sexual abuse, so it was all there in my medical r ecords."

"Oh, my God!" she breathes. "That's awful!"

"The doctors reported it to CPS, but something went wrong between the abuse report and the hospital and the social worker who came to get me. The guy didn't get the report or something like that. He took me back to the house and I ran away again three days later. I stayed away after that and I moved around a lot to make sure no one ever found out that I was living away from the house. The husband of this foster family had two grown sons—both in their late twenties. All three of them used to take me out to the garden shed. That's where they did it. The guy's wife drank a lot, so she either ignored it or didn't know about it. They had a teenage daughter who stayed out of her dad's and older brothers' way most of the time—so that left me. All three of the guys got convicted and they're all upstate doing time now. So that's pretty much the whole story."

She faces front. "I'm sorry I asked, Rory."

"I'm not." I grab her hand and squeeze. "I want you to know everything about me—just like you wanted me to know everything about you. We're a team here. You need to know if there's anything about me that could make me unsuitable for you as a partner."

"Unsuitable?!" She spins around to practically yell at me. "How could you say that about yourself? How could you ever be unsuitable for me as a partner?!"

"I'm not saying I am. I'm saying you need to know the facts so you can decide that for yourself. You're the reporter. Facts are supposed to be your bread and butter. I'm just telling you...."

She turns all the way around on her stool and snaps at me from the side. "Okay, here are the facts that I consider relevant to deciding if you're a suitable partner for me. Okay? Are you listening, Rory? First you told me I wasn't acting with journalistic integrity by publishing my first story without doing the research and interviewing the subjects before I made a bunch of unfounded accusations. Then you saved me at the hotel AND drove me home afterward AND offered to stay with me in case I didn't want to be alone—and that was after I slandered the club and everyone in it—including you. Are you with me so far? Then you wiped the slate clean and let me start over with no hard feelings after I corrected my mistake by defending the club."

"Well, yeah. Of course I did. You redeemed yourself."

"You've accepted everything about me—my mistakes, my background, my needs....You've given me everything and protected and taken care of me every time I've ever needed you to. You've given me all the grace I needed to make up for being a shitty reporter and a shitty person..."

"You were never a shitty person, sweetheart. You made a mistake. Everyone does it."

"Do you think I give a crap that you were abused as a kid and lived out of dumpsters?!" she counters. "Do you honestly believe I would use that as the metric for deciding if you were a suitable partner for me? I can't believe I'm hearing this."

"Well, it might be. It wouldn't be the first time."

She gapes at me in horror. "You can't be serious."

I shrug. "I'm just saying."

She turns back to her food and starts stabbing it with her knife and fork like she really does think it might still be alive. "Unbelievable," she snarls. "Flippin' unbelievable."

"I'm glad you think I'm a suitable partner for you. I'm sorry if I let past experience color my expectations."

"Well, it doesn't make you unsuitable as a partner for me—not at all. Let's just be clear on that right now. The preponderance of evidence on the other side of the scale is overwhelming, I would say. I don't see that your history comes into consideration at all since it's never affected our interactions with each other, but I would consider it inconsequential if it had come up. It's inconsequential compared to the dizzying array of evidence that suggests you would be more than a suitable partner for me. You would be an ideal partner for me. So th ere."

"Thank you," I murmur. "You're the first and only person I've ever met who feels this strongly about it."

"Well, I do," she snaps out the side of her mouth. "I'd like to get my hands on the people who convinced you otherwise."

I don't know what to say to her. No one has ever stuck up for me like this. Most scream and run in the other direction.

We finish eating breakfast. That didn't go the way I expected it to, either, but I'm glad we got it out in the open. I would never want to hide something like that from here.

She finishes first and starts cleaning up the kitchen while I lick the last of the sauce off my plate. She laughs at me, but she doesn't stop me. This sauce is mind-blowing.

She takes my plate—which is practically clean anyway—and puts everything in the dishwasher. "I'm going to have to cook for you more often," she tells me.

"That's what I said."

She rises on her tiptoes to kiss me. "Would you be able to give me a ride home so I don't have to take the subway?"

"Of course. Let's go."

I get my keys, phone, and laptop bag, lead her to the elevator, and we ride down to the parking garage where I put her in my car.

I drive her to her building. "Don't get out. I'll run inside. You go to work." She kisses me again. "I'll see you tonight, okay?"

"What time should I pick you up?"

"I finish work at five, so I would say any time after seven."

"I'll be here at seven-oh-one."

She laughs and gets out of the car blushing. She dashes across the street and vanishes into the building.

Chapter 26:
Nicole

I rush up the stairs to the *Record* office and get to my desk in time for my shift to start. I log onto my computer, hang my coat over the back of my chair, and put my purse under the desk before I realize that all is not well in the state of Denmark.

A bunch of people stand off to one side whispering to each other. The tension in the room vibrates at an epic pitch. No one talks back and forth across their desks to each other. No one hardly talks at all and those that do murmur or whisper.

I glance around, try one last time to ignore it, and realize something really is wrong.

"What's going on?" I ask May Quincy. She occupies the desk across from mine.

"Haven't you heard?" she breathes. "Cain Palmer is putting the *Record* up for sale. He says it isn't profitable anymore, so he's getting rid of it."

I blink at her. My conversation with Wayne comes back to haunt me. Is Cain Palmer selling the *Record* because of my story?

Enough time has passed since then. He should have offloaded the outlet when I published the story if he was going to do it at all. He should have at least gotten Wayne to fire me instead of keeping me on.

I try to get back to work, but the anxiety coming from my co-workers racks my nerves. I need answers—just like everyone else in the room.

I walk over to Wayne's office. He's sitting behind the desk. "Can I come in for a second, Wayne?" I ask.

"Sure," he replies over his shoulder. "What can I do for you?"

"Is Cain Palmer getting rid of the *Record* because of me? Is that what this is about? Is he retaliating against everyone because of my story? May said the decision was financial, but maybe he just said that to justify his actions."

He sighs and turns around to face me. "No, the decision had nothing to do with you. The *Record* has been losing money for years."

"How is that possible?" I think fast. I'm the one who has been doing the most research on Cain Palmer and Capitol Media Group these last few months. "None of Capitol's other news outlets are losing money—or is he getting rid of all of them?"

"No, it's only the *Record*. The others are all fine."

I frown to myself. Something about this doesn't make sense.

"Don't beat yourself up about it, sweetheart," Wayne tells me. "You're a good reporter. All of you will get good references. You'll get other jobs and keep doing your thing somewhere else. You have nothing to worry about."

I have too much on my mind, so I go back to my desk and continue doing research on my next story. I can't stop thinking about this, though.

I should dust off my resumé and start sending it around to other news outlets now. I should start making plans to take some unemployment time before I find another job. I need to check my finances and see about....well, everything.

I mean, I could move back home with my father in the absolute worst possible scenario. I'll never go without a roof over my head. I know he would be happy to have me back.

I don't want to do that, but I might have to. I can think of worse ways to live. Rory has already gone through it and look at him now. He definitely conquered that one.

I get through the day and go home to get ready to go out with him. I should put this out of my mind so I can concentrate on our date. I don't want to repeat that night at the Cloisters. That was a disaster.

I should do something to make it up to him, but he seems more than happy to let it slide.

He shows up at seven-oh-one exactly the way he said he would. He pretends to frown at his watch when I open the door. "Are you sure you're ready?" he asks. "I can wait a few more minutes—say until seven-oh-eight."

I laugh. "Quit fooling around. Let's get out of here."

We go outside, get into his car, and he heads north again. "Are we going back to the Cloisters?" I ask. "That was a really nice date. I'm sorry I ruined it for you."

"You didn't ruin it at all. It all went perfectly—and no, we aren't going back there. The weather is too cold."

He drives across town and parks in front of the Monarch Restaurant. It's a five-star culinary experience. The *Record* has covered it more than once.

"I should have dressed up more," I murmur on our way inside.

"You look fine. You always look outstanding. You especially looked outstanding in those work clothes I got to unpeel."

I blush and laugh. The host leads us to a quiet table by ourselves. Rory pulls my chair out for me and pours me a glass of wine. "This is beautiful," I exclaim. "Thank you in advance."

"You might really hate it. The chef might be terrible compared to your father. That is going to be a tough act to follow."

I smile at him and glance toward the kitchen. Remembering the stories the *Record* has run on this place reminds me of today's revelations.

Rory reads my mind in a heartbeat. That guy has some kind of sixth sense when it comes to anything bothering me.

"How was work today?" he asks.

I take a deep breath. "We found out today that Palmer is selling the *Record*. He says it's been losing money for years."

"Is that true or is he retaliating because of those stories you ran on him?"

"That's what I thought, but I asked Wayne and he says the outlet really is underwater. I never would have believed it, but I guess it really is true."

"Why would you never have believed it? Did you look into the *Record's* finances during your previous investigation?"

"No, I didn't have to, but Wayne says all of Capitol Media's other outlets are doing fine. All news outlets are online now. It isn't like any of them has any kind of paper distribution anymore—not to speak of. All the outlets make their money from online subscriptions—so it shouldn't technically be possible for one of them to do badly financially while all the others are doing well. The only difference between them is their coverage of local events. Outlets in New York cover New York events. Philly outlets cover Philly events and so on."

"Would the local coverage be enough to swing it one way or the other?"

"I might be willing to believe that except that we have the *Atlantic Connection* in New York, too. Both outlets are owned by Capitol and both outlets run New York local stories. So if the local coverage really was the critical factor, it should be affecting the *Connection* the same way—but it isn't."

He frowns at me. "That is strange."

I look away. "Anyway, it doesn't matter because I have to start looking for another job."

"What are your plans?"

I shrug at nothing. "The smart thing to do would be to update my resumé and start sending it out so I can start working somewhere either before the *Record* sells or immediately after Capitol lets us go. I've been thinking about it all day, but I haven't looked at my resumé even once. I don't know why."

He looks up at me. "Is there a reason why?"

I squirm under his scrutiny. "I'm not sure if I should tell you."

He snorts at me. "Sweetheart—please. You should never balk at telling me anything—especially not after our conversation this morning. Whatever it is you have on your mind can't possibly be worse than that."

I can't look at him. "You're a lot braver than I would be if I had to tell someone that."

"It doesn't require any bravery at all because it wasn't my fault. I had nothing to do with it except that I happened to be there at the time. I trust you with all my secrets. I'm sure whatever you have to tell me about your job isn't even something that could make me think you were unsuitable as a partner for me."

I try to laugh it off. "Maybe it would."

"Come on! Spit it out. I'm not going to stop nagging you until you tell me." He pretends to check his watch again. "I'll give you until the waiter brings our menus. You have to tell me before then....."

He breaks off when the waiter comes right then. We both laugh. The waiter gets confused and thinks we're laughing at him. Rory assures him that we aren't, but the guy doesn't believe him. The waiter takes our order and walks away steaming.

"Ouch," Rory exclaims. "I'm going to have to give him a huge tip."

"Remember when you told me I should apply for Wayne's job?"

Rory sits back in his chair. "Oh, I get it now."

"I mean.....what if I bought the *Record* and ran it myself?"

"You might want to check the books first."

"Well, I would have to check the books as part of the purchase process, wouldn't I? That would be a condition of the sale—that I get to examine exactly where the outlet is losing money."

"Wouldn't that all be electronic, too?" he asks.

"But what if it isn't? What if the money is disappearing somewhere else? What if the problem isn't a lack of subscriptions? How do you explain one outlet out of the entire Capitol Media Group losing money and none of the others? It makes no sense at all."

"You need to find that out before you start spinning off into all kinds of wild ideas like thinking you're going to buy the *Record*."

I think about it for a second. "Okay. I can do that."

He looks up at me. "You would seriously buy it? Are you sure?"

"Then I would have creative control over what we print and what we don't print. No one would be able to run any more malicious stories on The Billionaires' Club—or anyone else. I would be able to ensure that all my reporters did their jobs to the same high standard. I just don't have the money to buy the outlet."

"Don't you think you're jumping the gun just a little bit? You don't even know if the *Record* is a money-making venture. In fact, it sounds like it definitely isn't—and there's a lot more to running a business than just having the creative control to decide what stories to run."

I hesitate again. "Okay, tell me."

"Tell you what?"

"What does it take to run a business? What would I need to know to make it profitable—assuming it isn't and the money isn't accidentally taking a walk into someone's pocket somewhere along the way?"

He doesn't seem to hear me. He blinks at me across the table while the waiter puts our food in front of us.

"Are you serious?" Rory asks after the waiter leaves. "You actually want me to tell you how to run a business?"

"Yes, of course. Who better to learn from than someone who has already done it? What do I need to know?"

He clears his throat and adjusts his position in his seat. "I'm not sure I'm the best person to tell you that."

"Why not? You're already here right in front of me. I need help. I need to learn from someone and you're already right here. Who else would I ask?"

He looks away.

"What's wrong? Do you think I'm not smart enough to figure it out or something?"

"No, of course not. That isn't the reason at all."

"What is, then?"

"Melody said the same thing to Niko when she first inherited her father's fortune. He told me. He thought he should stay out of it because he thought his opinion would influence her and stop her from using her own judgment. He thought she should learn from other people in the club—people she wasn't in a relationship with. She convinced him by saying the same thing you just said right now—that he was the most accessible and could give her the information she needed without having to go to someone else."

"So will you do it? I really need someone who knows what they're doing."

"Well, the first thing you need is a unique value proposition."

"What does that mean?"

"It means you need to be offering something to the public that they can't get from anyone else. If the *Record* is losing money, I would say it's because the readers can already get exactly the same information from any of a dozen other sources, including the *Connection*. Capitol Media has more than five different news outlets in New York City alone and Capitol insists on all of them running the same generic, mediocre, boring, unremarkable stories. Capitol could easily combine all five of them into one outlet and accomplish the same thing. They would save money and the reader wouldn't know the difference."

I frown at him. "You're right. I didn't think of that."

"So if you were serious about taking on the *Record*, you would have to completely retool how you did things and what stories you ran. You would have to find a way to run completely different material from all the other Capitol outlets and all other news outlet on the internet. That's the only way to distinguish yourself and get readers coming to you for something they can't get anywhere else. That's what a unique value proposition is."

"Wow," I exclaim. "That's a lot to think about."

"And you want to think about your brand. The *Record* has no brand recognition right now. In fact, it has no brand at all. Capitol Media has a brand. It's known for exactly the kind of bland, mass-produced swill we see from every other news outlet. Capitol reprints everything else everybody else is reprinting and even the same old crap every other Capitol news outlet is reprinting. That's going to get you nowhere. You need brand recognition, brand awareness, and your brand has to actually stand for something. You have to have a reputation for excellence and for breaking new ground in ways no other outlet has the balls to do it. That's how you make money and attract people to pay for your product."

My hand flies to my head. "Wow. I don't even know how to think about that. The Capitol version of the news is all I've ever known."

"Maybe that's the problem." He looks down at his food and picks up his fork. "Let me know if you want any other information. Just remember the news business isn't my area of expertise. That's your j ob."

I lean forward. "I don't want you to swoop in and save the day by buying the *Record* like you did with my father's building. Okay? I want to make that clear. I don't want you to roll in and fix this for me."

"I wasn't planning to. I bought the building as a business investment—not an act of charity."

"How was it an investment? It isn't like my father's restaurant makes any money—and you wouldn't be getting any money from it even if it did make money."

"Your father's business wasn't the investment. The building was. Your father's restaurant is a tiny, no-name establishment in the basement. The rest of the building is commercial office space and even a few manufacturing operations and workshops. They're all high-value tenants with long, established leases and the building itself is structurally sound and well-maintained. The basement would be dead space if your father's restaurant wasn't there. It adds to the overall profitability of the whole building."

I frown to myself. "Oh. I didn't think about that." I shake that off. "Well, I don't want you to buy the *Record* on my behalf. I want to do it so I have control and I'm in charge of it. I just need to figure out how."

"Normally, when someone wants to start a business or buy a business they don't have enough money to purchase, they solicit investment from other people who do have the money."

My jaw drops. "What are you suggesting—that I roll up to a bunch of rich people and say, 'Hey, do you want to give me money to buy a news outlet?' Who would I ask—The Billionaires' Club?"

"They don't *give* you the money, sweetheart. They invest in the business in exchange for a share of the profits. You have to share your hard-earned profits with them on a percentage. They become part-owner side by side with you."

"And that gives them decision-making power over what content we produce, doesn't it?"

He shrugs. "Yes, it does. That's how these rich investors manipulate the news cycle to their advantage. That's exactly the problem we see in the news reporting field."

I shut my mouth in a hurry. "I don't want that. I don't want some random investor telling me what I can and can't print.'

"Then you need to come up with someone who does have the money and who you wouldn't mind taking that kind of input from. You need to think about people who actually have a stake in building this business and who share your values and want to pull toward the same goal."

My eyes fly open and I point at him. I almost jump out of my seat. "I got it! I could get all the other reporters together! We could buy the *Record*! They share my values and they all do have a stake in the business. They're all going to lose their jobs if the outlet closes. We would have to....." My mind goes into a tailspin. "Oh my God! I just had a brainwave."

"Uh-oh."

I ignore that. "Okay. How about this? The problem is that all these other outlets churn out the same mass-produced trash as every other outlet, so we have to do the opposite. We have to cut all the stories about cats caught in trees, people winning the lottery, and car crashes on the interstate. We have to become known for super high-quality, in-depth, investigative exposés. Every story has to be a scoop—an important, ground-breaking, seismic scoop that rocks the world by exposing something no one else can come up with. Everyone else is going for the low-hanging fruit, so we have to concentrate on material no one else will put in the effort to get." I clap my hands. "Yeah! This is going to be great. The other reporters can all get on board with that. We'll brand ourselves as a reporter co-op that prides itself on journalistic integrity, fearless investigation of the truth, and scrupulous adherence to established, verifiable fact. We'll pride ourselves on not allowing any outside investor to influence our decisions or our reporting standards. That will have to be one of the stipulations of investment—that the investor has no creative input at all."

He cocks his head to study me. "I think you should approach some of the club members anyway—not me, obviously, because I have a conflict of interest. I think you would find some very interested parties in the club."

"Really? Why would they be interested in a news outlet?"

"They would be interested in any business that prides itself on excellence and has a unique brand identity and market position that no one else is filling. You can't lose anything by talking to them about it. A project you're this passionate about is bound to fly—but you have to get the other reporters on board with it first. Don't forget that part of it."

I burst out in excited laughter. "I'm going to go for it! This is going to be great."

He leans back in his chair sipping his wine and watching me. "You might want to finish your dinner. You're going to need fuel to power that big brain of yours."

I get busy eating my food. I have a ton on my mind and a shitload of work to do, but he's right. I feel more passionate about this than I ever felt about working for the *Record* when it belonged to someone else.

I probably felt that way—or didn't feel that way—because the outlet didn't stand for anything. None of the stories meant anything, which meant *I* didn't stand for anything or mean anything, either.

The stories I ran on The Billionaires' Club were the only exceptions. I felt passionate about them because they did mean something to me and I *was* taking a stand on something.

What if every story could be like that? What if the whole outlet stood for that? What if every reporter in the whole company felt the same way and worked their asses off to make it happen? What if every dollar of profit meant that?

That would be something to work for. That would be something worth fighting for and getting out of bed for every morning. How can I have just been going through the motions all this time without that?

It doesn't matter because I'm going for it now. Any of the reporters who don't get on board with it will have to move on when the *Record* gets sold anyway.

It would be better to run the outlet with half or even a tiny fraction of the reporters instead of all that dead weight doing human interest stories on high-society socialites, celebrities, fashion shows, Broadway openings, and local construction projects and traffic delays.

We could actually be making a difference. We could actually be informing people about things they want and need to know about. We could be shedding light on events and problems and helping make the world a better place instead of being part of the problem.

I look up when I notice that Rory isn't eating anymore. He finished his food while I was going off about the *Record*.

"I'm sorry I'm so focused on myself tonight," I tell him. "I shouldn't have monopolized the conversation."

"No, you didn't. We've been having a very good conversation—and you obviously needed to talk about this. That's what I'm here for. I want to be the first person you talk to if you have something on your mind or you need help with something."

I point at him. "There. That right there. That's what makes you such a suitable partner for me."

He turns bright red and looks away. "Let's not start that all over again."

I hold out my hand across the table. "I'm in love with you. I don't want anyone but you."

His eyes go hard and he slips his hand into mine. "I'm in love with you, too. I'm madly, head-over-heels gone on you. I want you to move in with me and never leave."

I stiffen and then all resistance dies. "I want that, too."

"Are you sure you can stand to live on the Upper East Side? I wouldn't want you to compromise your professional standards."

I laugh. "I might have to move up the social ladder if I'm going to pivot from being a rank-and-file reporter to the managing editor of my own news outlet. I'm going to have an image to maintain."

He doesn't take the joke. "I have a question for you."

"Go ahead."

"My apartment—does it bother you?"

My head shoots up. "What?! No! Why would it? It's nice."

"Are you sure? I mean......you're dating a billionaire. Maybe you want to live the life and move into a mansion."

I snort at him and roll my eyes. "Are you on drugs? You should see the apartment where I grew up."

"I don't need to. I'm asking if you're okay with it the way it is or you want to upgrade."

"Your apartment *is* an upgrade, Rory."

"You know what I mean. It isn't what you might have expected from dating a billionaire."

I make a face. "I'm not dating a billionaire. I'm dating you. You have a beautiful apartment. Any girl would be delighted to live there with you."

He puts his wine glass down. "Maybe not any girl."

I don't comment that I know exactly what he means. I set my cutlery on one side of my plate. "I'm ready to go whenever you are."

He pays the check and we get into his car. We hold hands and exchange glances on the drive back to his place. "Did you bring your blow-drier this time?" he asks.

I laugh. "I didn't have room in my purse, but I did bring a toothbrush and an extra pair of panties."

"Would you like to stop by your place and pick up a few things?"

I turn around to stare at the side of his face. "You would do that?"

He answers by flipping a U-turn at the next stoplight and motoring back south toward my apartment. "You should have said something when I picked you up," he tells me. "You could have left a bag in the back of the car."

"I would have said something if I had only thought of it first."

He parks in front of the building and walks me up to my apartment. I lead the way inside and shut the door behind him. I'm just about to rush off to pack, but he catches me and pulls me into his arms. "Move in with me," he whispers. "I don't ever want to let you go."

"I want that," I murmur back. "I don't want us to be apart. You're the best thing that has ever happened to me."

He leans forward, shuts his eyes, and rests his forehead against mine. His voice breaks in a tortured undertone. "You're the only person who has ever said that about me."

I can't stop kissing him all over his face. "You're perfect—in every way. You're the best man I could ever hope for. Don't you know I wake up every morning wondering how I can be good enough for you?"

He shakes his head. "I'm the one...."

"You're wrong. You're the standard. Don't you know that? You're the standard I want to live up to. You always have been. You've always been the example for me to follow. You're the one with integrity. You're the one who taught me that." I kiss him on the forehead. "Now come on. I gotta get my stuff so we can go home together."

Chapter 27:
Nicole

R ory sits up on the edge of the bed and takes his phone off the bedside table. I roll in his direction and run my hand up and down his bare back while he checks his notifications.

"You're beautiful," I murmur.

"You're beautiful," he replies over his shoulder.

"You're sexy," I tell him.

"Don't start that," he counters. "Don't you ever sleep? How do you expect to function today when I've been up all night making your toes curl?"

I sit up and kiss him on the shoulder. Then I rub my breasts up and down his arm. "Would you like to do it again before work?"

He doesn't look away from his phone. "I can see that I'm going to have to be the grownup in this relationship. I'm going to have to be the one who tells you when it's time to stop because you sure as hell won't."

I flop back on the bed, take hold of his hand, and move it back and forth across my breasts. "I can't help it if I find you irresistible."

He squeezes, massages, and flicks my nipples without stopping what he's doing. He uses the button click noise on his phone so I can hear every time he taps out a letter in a message or email.

He teases my breasts for a while and doesn't stop working with his left hand while I move his right hand down between my legs to touch me. He circles his flattened fingers on my clitoris and then trails his fingertips through my swollen, sensitive petals.

Doing it with him all night makes me extra turned on by the slightest touch. He still doesn't react when I moan and seethe under his hand.

He doesn't look up until he puts his phone back on the bedside table. Then he turns around, buries his face between my legs, and gives me a dozen deep, mouth-watering bites and licks to electrify me.

He sits up almost immediately. "I'm going to take a shower now. Then I'm going to get dressed while you take a shower and get ready for work. You're going to go into the office and talk to all your co-workers and fellow reporters about investing their hard-earned savings to turn the *Record* into an investigative reporter co-op. I suggest you use the time while I'm in the shower to think about what you're going to say to convince them instead of playing with yourself and fantasizing about me."

He gives me one pointed look and walks off toward the bathroom. Dang. Now I really am thinking about how to convince them.

He sure knows how to throw a bucket of cold water over me. I probably would have spent the time playing with myself and fantasizing about him if he hadn't just said that. Now I can't think about anything other than talking to my fellow reporters.

This whole project gets me fired up and driven to make it happen. I'm already out of bed getting ready to start my day by the time he comes out of the shower with his hair wet and a towel wrapped around his waist.

Seeing him with his clothes off makes me insatiably hungry for him, but that will have to wait. It's adult time right now.

I take a shower, get dressed for work, and do my hair in front of the mirror. Rory is in the kitchen by the time I get out to the living room.

He's running the blender to make himself a smoothie. "Where's mine?" I ask.

"Over there." He points to the counter where he's laid out a breakfast of fried eggs on buttered toast with four strips of bacon, hashbrowns, and a small pile of assorted fruit.

"Hey!" I exclaim. "You said you didn't know how to cook."

"I don't call this cooking. Waving a few basic staples in the general direction of the stove doesn't qualify as cooking."

"This is great." I sit down in front of my plate. "You should have made some for yourself."

"I don't usually eat solid food for breakfast. I almost always have this."

I smirk at him. "I do, too, actually. We'll have to save the gourmet breakfasts for special occasions and the mornings after date nights."

He catches my eye and looks away. "Do you need help with anything today?" he asks. "Do you feel on top of everything?"

"Yeah, I'm feeling pumped about it. I wanted to ask you what you meant when you used the word, 'approach' when you talked about soliciting investment from the club members. How would I do that? Do you mean cold emailing them, asking them to meet with me—how do I do it?"

He takes a sip of his smoothie while he thinks it over. "Probably the best way would be to set up a meeting with several of them. Then you can present your pitch, tell them what you're offering and what you're asking for them in return, and see what they say. They'll probably ask a lot of questions and make comments about it."

"How do I set up the meeting? Do I contact each of them separately and invite them to come hear my pitch?"

"That's one way of doing it."

"What are the alternatives?"

"I could let them know about it. We have a club meeting today. I could put it on the agenda."

"You already said it would be a conflict of interest for you to get involved."

"I wouldn't do it as your boyfriend or whatever it is I am. I would do it in my role as the club's PR officer. I would point out that investing in this project could be the best thing for the club since you've already shown yourself to be an ally of the club. I could point out that this new outlet promises to be one of the very few sources of unbiased information that can present a positive image to the world of what the club is trying to accomplish. I could point out that partnering with you would promote our interests. That kind of integrity and professional standard is exactly the kind of business we should be supporting."

"But....won't it come out that we're dating—or whatever it is we're doing?"

He shrugs. "It will probably come out at some point—if not then, then soon."

"And....are you okay with that?"

"I'm more than okay with it. I want them to find out. I'm proud of you. I told you that. You're the one I want to be with. You're the one I want everyone to see me with. This project is just one more reason why I want the whole world to know."

Now I'm the one who looks away. "You're the only person who has ever felt that way about me."

"I'm sure your family feels that way about you."

"They don't count. They're family."

He sidles around behind my stool and buries his face in my neck from behind. "That's what I want us to be, sweetheart. I want us to be that close and connected. I want it all. I don't want to be in any category other than in the stands with your biggest fans. Now come on. You need to get your fellow reporters on board before I talk to the club about anything."

He puts on his jacket. I get my purse and all my devices. We go downstairs and get into his car so he can drive me to work.

"I'll call you at lunchtime to see how much progress you're making in convincing your colleagues to get on board with this," he tells me. "If you're making progress and things are looking good, I'll bring up the subject at our meeting. I'll make a time when anyone who is interested can get together with you and hear your pitch. Okay?"

I puff out my cheeks to steady my nerves. "Okay! I can do that."

He squeezes my hand. "You're gonna be great. Go knock their socks off, tiger."

He kisses me outside the building and I go inside. Now it's crunch time.

Chapter 28:
Nicole

The *Record* is in an uproar when I get upstairs. No one is getting any work done anymore.

Everyone stands around talking about the outlet going up for sale. Speculation and anxious murmurs fly back and forth about who might buy the *Record* and whether the new owners will keep on any of the journalism staff.

A bunch of people are already sending out resumés and even interviewing at other outlets to try to find jobs. A few people are even talking about quitting journalism altogether.

I'm just putting my purse down on my desk when Mael comes around to tell us that Wayne is calling us to a staff meeting in fifteen minutes. The announcement sets off another shockwave of anxiety and nervous agitation among the staff. This is not good.

The whole journalism and office staff files into the meeting room. Only a handful of people can fit in the chairs around the table. The rest of us have to pack against the walls.

Wayne elbows his way to the front of the room and turns around to address us. "You all know I was planning to retire at the end of the month. I just got word that the company is suspending my employment effective immediately. I'll be going home after this meeting and I won't be coming back. You won't get another managing editor until the company sells and someone else takes over."

"So what are we supposed to work on until then?" someone asks. "Are we supposed to keep working on our current assignments?"

"I can't answer that because I'm not your managing editor anymore," Wayne replies. "I'm not anyone's editor or an editor at all. I'm retired. I don't think any of you should be working on any stories right now. I think you all need to go back to your desks and start updating your resumés if you haven't done it already. I think you should take advantage of this time to find employment and a source of income for your families. That's what I would be doing right now if I was in your shoes. You've all been a wonderful staff and I've enjoyed every minute of working here. I wish each and every one of you the best. Any of you can let me know and I'll write you a recommendation for your next position."

He starts working his way back through the mob toward the door to leave the room. A ripple of agitation follows him. Everyone exchanges glances and murmurs back and forth that we're all effectively out of a job now.

A few other people head for the exit, too. "Wait!!" I call out. "Don't leave yet! I have something I want to say!"

A bunch of people turn around. Everyone watches me shoulder my way to the front of the room. My heart starts racing when I face the staff.

"The *Record* is not underwater financially!" I announce. "The *Record* has the same number of ongoing subscriptions, the same number of staff, and the same expenses as every other Capitol Media news outlet. The *Connection* also operates in New York and even pays a higher rent for its office premises and that outlet isn't underwater. I looked into it and it turns out that someone on the Capitol Media executive board has been embezzling money from the company for years. The person has been siphoning funds from the *Record's* accounts and diverting them to a separate offshore account to make it look like the *Record* was in trouble when it wasn't."

This causes another buzz of excited murmurs and raised eyebrows.

"I propose that we band together and purchase the *Record* as an investigative reporter co-op that is jointly owned and operated by all of us," I go on. "We would all invest in buying the company, we would all contribute to creative decisions, and we would all bring a level of commitment and integrity that this company is sorely lacking. The Capitol Media brand is boring, lackluster, and totally devoid of any professional standard. The whole chain prints and reprints the same meaningless nonsense and throwaway pieces across every outlet. It's a miracle anyone subscribes to our platform at all. We could change that. We could become known for breaking new ground, scooping information no one else has the courage to uncover, and influencing the world in a positive way. The Capitol brand has become known for corporate interests using their money and power to twist the news for their own ends. We could be the change we want to see by stopping that and becoming known as the one outlet that sticks to the facts. That would be our unique offering—that we present our findings with the impartiality and integrity we should have been giving them all this time. We don't have to be cogs in the machine. We can make the *Record* into something great instead of something cookie-cutter and forgettable."

"You're crazy!" one man yells from the back. "That will never work."

I square my shoulders at the whole crowd and throw back my head. "I'm doing this with you or without you. If you don't believe in this mission, then you can all go back to your desks and start working on your resumés and making phone calls. Any of you that want to join me are more than welcome. It would be better for three or four of us to work on this with all our hearts and energy than for us to drag along anyone who doesn't believe in the mission and isn't committed to the same standard. No one will be sorry when you leave. Trust me on that."

Dead silence answers me. I don't care anymore if I convinced them or not. I don't want anyone around who isn't one hundred percent on board with this.

We might take a hit in income. We might not make any money at first. We all might wind up working for free until word spreads about what we're trying to accomplish here.

I can live with that. Everyone who joins me better be ready for that, too.

I refuse to take anyone who doesn't share that level of commitment. We all have to pull together with equal enthusiasm for the core values this project is going to require.

Almost everyone leaves the room. Five people come up to me at the front.

"I'm with you, Nicole," Hugo Bond tells me. "The *Record* has been a dead-end operation for years."

"This is going to be the best way for us to take back creative control," Brody Gomez adds. "We'll be able to choose our own stories instead of someone else telling us what to write."

"It's almost like Capitol Media was actively trying to ignore the important stories and telling us to work on the meaningless ones," Poppy Metzenger chimes in. "Did you ever notice that? Why else would they dedicate so much space to fluff pieces and car crashes?"

"The tricky part is going to be scraping together the funds to purchase the business," I tell them. "I have some savings and I'm soliciting a few investors, but the more investment funds come from us, the less we'll need from other sources."

A few different people interject by telling me how much they have saved and how much they would be able to get if this project goes ahead.

Everyone else leaves the room while the six of us spend the next half an hour in the meeting room talking and firing ideas back and forth. We have a ton to talk about and everyone gets progressively more amped up the longer we talk about it.

Five people—six including me. That's plenty. Now we just need the money. I make a note of how much everyone wants to contribute.

Then I do a quick search on my phone and find out how much Capitol is asking for the business. We're nowhere even close to being able to purchase it, but I don't tell my core group of supporters that.

I send them all out to their desks with orders to start researching our first stories. Most of these people are going to have to get other jobs to support their families while they work on the *Record* on the side.

I reassure them all that we'll be extremely flexible with everyone's schedules from now on. It's going to take time for this business to gain traction.

The whole point of the co-op is that we work the business around our own needs. We're all going to be joint owners in the project, so we can adjust it to fit our lives and really put in the time and effort the project needs to grow.

We also agree to include as a condition of the sale that Capitol gives us the *Record's* email list of subscribers.

We plan to email everyone ahead of time to promote the new venture, explain what we're trying to do, and to encourage them to come on the journey with us. That should help a lot.

We all have to force ourselves to stop talking about this. We agree to meet one night a week at some casual location—like the Castle Brewery.

That's where we'll do all our strategic planning, brainstorming, and making big decisions about the direction we want to take the business.

We all leave the meeting room super excited about the road ahead. It's already past noon by the time we leave and Rory calls me.

"How's it looking?" he asks.

"It's great! I got five people! Isn't that wonderful? They're all super pumped. This is gonna be so awesome!" I give him a rundown on the decisions and plans we've made so far.

"Wow," he exclaims. "That's so much better than I expected."

"We are going to need investors. Do you still think the club is the way to go?"

"Yes, absolutely. I'll raise the issue at our meeting this afternoon and see who bites. It will be like it was with your co-workers. You don't need everyone. Just a few key people who believe in the project will be plenty."

"Thank you so much! I can't thank you enough."

"You can pay me back with sexual favors."

I laugh and we get off the phone. I have so much to do. This is going to be huge.

Chapter 29: Rory

I meet Nicole outside the boardroom at People, Inc. Kevin has agreed to let us use this boardroom to hear Nicole's pitch to buy the *New York Record*.

Kevin is here to act as our host, but he's already stated that he won't be investing in the project. He's already investing as much as he can afford in expanding People, Inc. into overseas markets.

Nicole shows up all out of breath and flushed with excitement. She kisses me in the hallway and casts a glance into the room behind me. "Are they preparing the firing squad?"

"It isn't like that. There are five guys in there—Judah, Lane, Giovanni, Niko, and Kevin. Kevin is only here as our host. He isn't a potential investor."

She nods. "You told me."

"And I'll be here. I won't be able to contribute, not even to support you. I'm the facilitator. That's all."

"I got that. Thank you for doing this. I'm really grateful."

"Are you ready to rock and roll?"

She blushes and nods. "Let's go."

I lead her into the room and sit on my side of the table. She's about to sit alone on her side of the table when two other men show up. She stands back up to greet them.

The three of them go off to the other side of the room and exchange a few nods and whispered snatches of conversation before they come back.

Everyone shakes hands with everyone else and introduces themselves. "Thank you all for coming to talk to us," Nicole begins. "This is Hugo Bond and this is Brody Gomez. The three of us have been empowered by the other three members of our cooperative to negotiate on their behalf and come to any agreement we come to."

"It's a pleasure to meet you all," Kevin tells her. "Take a seat and tell us what you have going on here."

All nine of us sit down. This feels much more balanced with three of them on that side of the table instead of just Nicole by herself.

She starts in on her pitch, explains what the *Record* has been until now, its history, and the new direction that she and her colleagues want to take it.

She's explicitly clear that the six co-op members will be equal partners. Instead of a managing editor the *Record* has had in decades past, the six of them will be acting as an editorial board to make business, strategic, and creative decisions for the outlet.

She outlines a structure whereby new people coming in will work for the co-op as employees for a minimum of two years before they're given an opportunity to join the co-op.

She says the decision to offer someone a place in the co-op will be entirely at the editorial board's discretion based on the person's previous job performance, integrity, and commitment to the co-op's mission and shared values.

She speaks fluently and passionately about this project. It's obvious from her energy that she believes in it and plans to do it with the billionaire's investment or without it.

She finishes her presentation and Hugo starts talking. He presents a truckload of information on the *Record's* financial situation and everything he and Nicole have been digging up about embezzlement by the Capitol Media executive board that makes it look like the outlet is underwater when it isn't.

He then presents spreadsheets, projections, and budgets for the business going forward. He obviously knows his stuff when it comes to crunching the numbers on any business. I haven't heard such a thorough and professional presentation in a long time.

He shows us different sets of projections. The first is based on the *Record's* past financial performance. The outlet has always employed more than thirty journalism staff and almost fifteen office staff.

He's retooled the projections based on only five journalism staff, cut the office staff to three, and adjusted the expense spread based on renting a much smaller premises to accommodate the smaller staff.

The outlet's subscriber base has been flat for years, so he bases these projections on the assumption that it will continue to stay flat.

He suggests that the subscriber numbers will drop when the co-op takes over and switches to the new business model. Then he proposes that the numbers will rise as word spreads and more people get interested in the co-op's content.

These numbers make the business much more profitable and much more attractive to any investor. I find myself evaluating the *Record* as an investment opportunity even though I won't be investing in it.

I'm really starting to wish I could invest in it. I wish I could support this project. It's important—and it stands to be very profitable if he's right about word of mouth growing the business over time.

Then he shows his second set of projections. These are similar but with one crucial difference. He proposes that the co-op completely eliminate all salaries for all the journalist co-op members. He proposes switching the co-op to a strictly profit-sharing model.

This means that no one in the co-op will draw any income from the business unless and until it turns a profit. None of the founding co-op members, the new members who join, or the investors will make a penny until the outlet starts to grow and bring in more funds.

This makes the startup financials look completely different. For one thing, the extra cash the business does bring in will make it break even sooner. The co-op will have to invest less to make the business profitable, which means they'll start earning sooner.

They also stand to earn a hell of a lot more in the long run. It's a powerful, visionary strategy that sends a shiver up my spine.

This is the kind of thing true believers come up with. The co-op members are willing to sink everything into this. They're willing to work other jobs on the side to pay the bills while they burn the midnight oil to launch this thing.

This is the sign that the people behind it are ready, willing, and fully committed to going the distance. They don't need us. They're going to do this whether they get investors or not.

Hugo shows us a third spread of projections based on the co-op members not hiring any office staff and not renting any premises. They plan to work from home and do all their own admin to make the company even more profitable until it gets off the ground.

There is absolutely no doubt in my mind that this venture will succeed. It can't possibly fail with this kind of drive and commitment behind it.

Brody speaks next and goes over some of the stories the co-op members are currently researching and investigating as their original startup content.

The co-op plans to prepare these stories and promote them leading up to the sale and right around the time when the newly rebranded *Record* launches.

The story content leaves the prospective investors speechless. The whole presentation leaves them speechless. Brody thanks everyone for their time and attention before he sits down. No one on our side of the table answers for a long time.

"Wow," Lane finally breathes. "Just...wow."

I see the way the wind is blowing, so I take that opportunity to stand up and hold out my hand to Nicole and her fellow reporters. "Thank you all for coming in to talk to us. I think we need to take some time to consider your proposal. You've given us a lot to think about. Let us go over all the information and we'll be in touch very soon, I'm sure."

We all shake hands. The other billionaires wake up from their shock, thank the three reporters, and Nicole and the others leave together.

"I'm in," Lane blurts out as soon as the door closes. "I don't know about the rest of you, but I'm in. This is....just.....wow. I mean....I have never heard anything like this. I have never—*ever*—heard such an excellent pitch. This is beyond anything I've ever seen or heard."

"I'm in, too," Giovanni adds. "This thing is gonna be big. It has to be. It's going to grow so much faster than they realize. The public is starving for this kind of authenticity and transparency. I almost wish I could buy it from them, but it's their personal commitment that makes it so great."

"I really wish I could invest in it," Kevin remarks. "This is important. This could revolutionize the whole profession of journalism."

"Let's hope it does," Judah chimes in. "I believe in the project, but this doesn't fit my profile for the kinds of businesses I'm looking to invest in. I'm only looking for established businesses that are already doing a certain amount in revenue. This is too small. It's hardly even a startup. It's just an idea."

"What about you, Niko?" Giovanni asks. "Are you in?"

"I think I will. I normally wouldn't invest in anything this small, either, but the potential for doing some good in the world makes it worthwhile for me. I'm in, too."

Kevin turns to me. "Will you be investing in it? Is that why you brought it to our attention?"

"No, I won't be investing in this project," I reply. "I brought it to your attention because I thought it was important for the club to invest in a totally impartial news outlet. Nicole has already shown us that she's committed to factual, impartial reporting. We need more of that. The club needs more of that."

"You could still invest in it," Lane points out. "I'm surprised you didn't put your money where your mouth is if you think it's so important."

I take a deep breath. I came into this meeting knowing it would come to this.

"I can't invest in the project," I tell them. "I wish I could, but I have a conflict of interest."

"What do you mean?" Kevin asks.

"Nicole and I are in a relationship. We've been going out for a while now. I'll be supporting the business another way. I can't invest financially."

"No way!" Lane exclaims. "Wow! Congratulations, man!"

Kevin shakes my hand and then the others all do it, too. Giovanni grins at me. "She's a lucky girl."

"So am I," I mumble. "She isn't what we thought she was at the start."

"She *was* that way at the start," Judah points out. "She changed—for the better."

Niko raises his eyebrows and puffs out his cheeks. "I never thought we would be sitting across from her in a meeting like this. She doesn't even seem like the same person she was back then."

"She isn't—or maybe she just forgot who she was for a little while. She's....she's special. I don't want to miss what could be the best thing I've found yet."

My friends gather around me congratulating me and telling me to bring her to the next gala. No one talks about the co-op proposal anymore. It's a done deal.

Chapter 30: Nicole

R ory shoots me a grin before he gets out of his car in front of the
Four Seasons Hotel. He opens my door for me, helps me out,
and hands his keys to the valet before escorting me inside.

"This should be a very different experience from your last gala," he
tells me on the way in.

I groan. "Can we somehow arrange to purge it from everyone's
memory banks?"

"No way. Everyone wants to remember so we can all admire how
much you've grown and changed since then. Give everyone a chance
to respect and admire the work you're doing."

I don't have time to answer before we glide into the ballroom. I
don't have time even to glance around at the servers before a bunch of
the billionaire club members and their wives surround us.

It doesn't matter if one of the servers spikes my drink tonight
because I don't plan on leaving Rory's side even for an instant. I'm
not risking that or anything even remotely like it.

A bunch of the billionaires start talking to Rory. Paige and Melody
come up on my other side, grab my other hand, and kiss me on the

cheek. "You didn't give us the chance to invest in you!" Melody tells me. "I feel cheated."

"How's the new munchkin?" I ask. "I'm surprised to see you out in public. I thought you would be in a sleep-deprived coma by now."

She laughs. "That's Niko. He's doing all the sleep deprivation for both of us."

"Seriously, Nicole," Paige exclaims. "I want to invest in the *Record*, too."

"Sorry, ladies, but we're closed to outside investment now. We got all we needed from Lane, Niko, and Giovanni. We only wanted enough to purchase the business. We don't want to share our profits with any more people."

"That is so not fair!" Melody counters. "You should have told all of us."

"Rory said he announced it at the club meeting," I point out. "You might not have been there, but Paige was."

Paige pretends to pout. "I didn't know it was going to be this. He didn't tell us enough."

"Just admit it. You missed the boat," Melody tells her. "You'll have to catch the next one."

"There never will be a next one," Paige points out. "This is the only journalist co-op I've ever heard of."

Piper Legrange, Mila Knapp, and Emberlynn Rhinehart gather around just then, but not before Lane and Niko elbow their way through the group.

They both kiss me on the cheek. "How are you feeling after submitting your offer to purchase the company?" Niko asks.

"I'm a nervous wreck. See this?" I hold up my hand. "I've been chewing my fingernails down to the bone and we only just submitted the offer a few hours ago. I know I won't hear anything until next week at the earliest, but I probably would have spent the evening sitting at home staring at my email inbox. Rory had to threaten me to leave the apartment."

They all laugh. "They'll accept your offer," Lane tells me. "I'm certain of it."

"They better because I can't take much more of the strain."

"I have a potential story for you, Nicole," Piper tells me.

I raise my eyebrows. "Really? Hit me with it."

"Former Deputy NYPD Chief Taylor Easterman is running for New York State Senate."

I frown at her. "Easterman. I recognize that name from somewhere."

"He was Deputy Chief of Police when the city charged Diego Espinosa with murder," Melody tells me. "Piper did some digging and traced the order to Easterman. The department scapegoated Jocelyn's commanding officer. He never told anyone who he got the order from, but Piper found a paper trail leading back to Easterman."

"No one has ever written up the whole story of the department trying to frame Diego," Piper adds. "You guys should look into it."

"I definitely will. Thanks for the tip."

"No one has ever written up the story of Spiderware CEO Demetrius Runyon stealing the original software code from the developer in his high school computer science class and murdering the kid in an alley with multiple stab wounds to the chest, either," Paige adds. "You should write that one up, too."

I gasp and my eyes fly open. "No way! I never heard that!"

"That's exactly why you should write it up," Emberlynn tells me. "It sure does seem like the mainstream press goes out of its way to pull the wool over everyone's eyes about this stuff."

Rory gets my attention just then by turning toward us and sticking his head between me and the others. "Excuse me, ladies. I'm going to steal Nicole from you for a minute."

"Just for a minute?" Emberlynn teases. "Don't lie, Rory."

He laughs and leads me deeper into the ballroom. I meet people I know and like everywhere I turn. All the club members and their wives come over to greet me and talk about....well, everything.

They talk about their businesses. They talk about their investments. They talk about the *Record*. They talk about the news. They talk about stories they've heard and that they think the co-op would be interested in.

It's like this every time I set foot outside the apartment where Rory and I live together now. The co-op has only just made its offer to buy the *New York Record*, but the business is already exploding off the charts.

We've taken over the outlet's website and started posting our new content. We've offered that the outlet's domain name and brand identity be included in the sale so we can keep the same name.

We've changed everything else about the business, including the logo, letterhead, fonts, and website layout. We've done all of this on our own without paying any other professional to do it for us.

We've also used the Capitol Media email marketing platform to announce to the rest of the parent company's subscriber base that the *Record* is going independent. We've used the same emails to inform the subscribers of what we're doing and how we'll be changing things.

Dozens of Capitol's subscribers have migrated to the *Record* and joined our mailing list. We're getting new subscribers by the day and we haven't even officially opened our doors yet.

We've even gotten some of Capitol's subscribers who've switched to the *Record* and canceled their Capitol subscription entirely. Hugo projects that we'll be turning a profit by the time we conclude the purchase and go out on our own.

I'm feeling giddy and shaky about the whole project. It's spiraling into something so much bigger than I thought it would. The public is obviously desperate for this kind of information.

I thought it would be harder to come up with subject matter to write our stories about. I didn't think these kinds of in-depth investigations would come up often enough to support an entire business.

Now I'm finding out that the opposite is the case. There seems to be a whole shadow world of intrigue and skullduggery going on behind the scenes that no one knows about. The mainstream press doesn't dare to touch this material with a ten-foot pole.

I'm starting to think Emberlynn is right. The news outlets take up the vast majority of their space with stories about stray dogs getting pulled out of storm drains so the outlets can claim they don't have space to run these other more in-depth pieces.

We've been fielding countless emails from our subscribers with information, stories, tips, and suggestions on investigations they want us to run.

Brody has suggested that we set up a special hotline email address where people can write in and tip us off about anything they hear or that they think we might be interested in.

We've started holding our weekly strategy meetings at each other's homes instead of going out. We all bring food and snacks and relax in a much more casual atmosphere.

We sit around talking late into the night. We don't have to worry about the management kicking us out or taking up a table someone else wants to use.

We've held a few of these meetings at the apartment I share with Rory. The other co-op members have families and children who don't want our noise to disturb them.

Rory makes himself scarce for these meetings. He teasingly refers to us a terrorist cell and doesn't want to hear about your next assassination attempt or subway bombing.

He's on friendly terms with all the co-op members now. I've gotten to know and made friends with a bunch of the other members' spouses and even some of their kids. The co-op is turning into a family. We're all in this and we all believe in it.

The co-op's early success gives us new energy and more inspiration than we can reasonably follow up on at any given time. We have to prioritize and even shift some of our better ideas to the back burner for now.

Our three investors have been outstanding, especially Giovanni. He's been using his contacts in the media world to promote us through his own platform. He's been announcing the development and impending launch of the *Record* as an alternative news outlet.

He's been helping us come up with a few different alternate funding models so we don't have to take advertising dollars from any company that might try to leverage our stories in their favor.

We haven't figured out a way to do it yet. If we mention any company by name, our readers will automatically think we're endorsing them. Mentioning anyone in our publication will make the reader assume the company is manipulating us.

The only alternative is to take anonymous donations, but the readers could even take that the wrong way. They could still assume the wrong thing the same way people assume donors are influencing colleges and universities.

The subscription model is still looking like the best option. We're talking about expanding our platform to video, documentaries, and other outlets.

Rory and I get drinks and nibbles. We stand in one place talking to one person after another. We both turn to separate groups. I don't have to keep my hand on his arm the whole time as long as he can see me and I can see him.

I see myself moving effortlessly in this world now. I know everyone and everyone knows me. Everyone remembers our rocky shared past, but no one mentions it.

They won't forget it and neither will I. That memory will be enough to keep me on the straight path from now on. I never want to fall that far again—and I won't as long as I have these people to keep me honest. I don't want to let them down.

Chapter 31: Rory

I 'm sitting on the couch in my shirtsleeves working on my laptop when Nicole comes in from work. She's been out doing interviews and tracking down sources all morning.

She leans over the back of the couch to kiss me. "Hey, sweetie. How's your day going?"

"Pretty good. How about you?"

"Pretty good. By the way, my father called me today. He asked if we could go to the restaurant for our next date night. He wants to see you."

I look up. "He does? Why?"

"He didn't say. He said he likes you and I should bring you there this weekend—or you should bring me there. I told him you've probably already made reservations somewhere, so we can go there next Saturday if you want to."

"This isn't a setup for another practical joke, is it?" I ask.

She grins at me. "I don't think so. I think he really likes you. He said we should come to the restaurant for dinner more often."

"I guess we could do that. I haven't made any reservations anywhere yet, so we can go there tonight. I guess we don't need a reservation to go there." I turn back to my screen. "Did you tell him what I said about the building needing natural disaster retrofitting? He has to close the restaurant for three days at the end of the month while the construction crew works in the basement."

"I told him. He's fine with it." She plops down next to me on the couch and folds her legs under her. "Whatcha working on?"

"I'm going over my asset portfolio for my end-of-year meeting with my financial advisor."

She squints at the screen. "North Star Investment Consultation Service. That's Judah Hayes's company."

I grin at her. "Could you stop investigating everything? What difference does it make who does it?"

"So how is your asset portfolio looking?"

"It's good. I need to rearrange a few things—nothing serious."

"That tip Piper gave me on the Easterman Senate campaign is blowing up into a full-scale tornado. We're going to have to send out a federal emergency warning pretty soon."

"Is he freaking out because you're looking into this?"

"He's doing more than freaking out. He tried to get an injunction to stop us from publishing any record of his term as Deputy Chief of the New York City Police Department. Can you believe the nerve? He's running for public office, for Christ's sake, and he wants to bar us from publishing anything about his previous conduct in public office. How stupid do you have to be? He's making himself look terrible. We won't even have to discredit him in the public press. He's doing it himself."

"It sounds like he has a lot more to hide than just implicating an innocent man in a murder charge."

"Exactly. Implicating Diego could have been the most innocuous thing he did as deputy chief."

I close my laptop and put my arm around her. "When do you want to go out tonight?"

"Don't we have a standing date for eight o'clock?"

"We can go early if you want to. We don't have to wait that long. I wouldn't want to interfere with your beauty rest."

She laughs at me and stands up. "I think I'll go start getting ready. I want to have plenty of time."

I do a few more things on my computer, put it away, and go into the bedroom to get ready to go out. I have a lot on my mind with my financial planning meeting coming up. I keep thinking about the future.

I keep getting these rushes of anxiety that I won't be ready financially for all I want to do, now that I have Nicole in my life. I know I will be ready, but I can't help dwelling on it.

I haven't felt like this in a long time. I've gotten used to having enough because it's always been just me by myself. The future looks different when I have a woman in my life.

I'm getting dressed in front of the dresser mirror when she comes out of the bathroom. She deliberately, teasingly uses her ass to bump me out of the way so she can get in front of the mirror instead.

I give her a smack on the backside before I go into the bathroom to do my hair.

She takes a long time to get ready. She always does, but I'm used to it by now. I love that she takes so much care for me. She doesn't care who looks at her as long as she's out with me.

No one will see her at her father's restaurant. I'll be the only one who gets to look at her, but she takes extra time to make sure she gets everything perfect before we leave.

She rests her hand on my shoulder while I drive south to Little Italy. She smiles at the view outside her window. I love seeing her happy and contented.

She's been so much happier since she and her friends took over the *Record*. They're all so much more enthusiastic and the investors are thrilled with the way the project is progressing.

The readers seem thrilled, too. The six reporters carry on a lively exchange with their readers about every story, every piece they publish, every idea one of the readers writes in about, and how the whole project keeps growing and building on itself.

Having such an engaged, invested readership gives all the reporters incredible energy. I would be very surprised if any other news outlet is getting this kind of engagement.

It's almost like it's supposed to be this way—that the readers are part of the family and part of the project. They're the real investors.

I park outside her father's restaurant, set my car alarm, and she takes my arm on the way downstairs. We walk into the usual succulent smells coming from the kitchen. We're the only people in here as usual.

Nicole and I come here every now and then for dinner, but not very often. We could definitely start coming more often. She's so comfortable here and having the place to ourselves feels nice. It's better than having to talk over a bunch of other people.

Her father comes out to greet us. He actually hugs me and makes me blush by kissing me on both cheeks. Nicole won't stop beaming at us.

She orders for both of us and I take her hand across the table after he leaves us alone. "Has Judah been your financial advisor for a long time?" she asks.

"Since I got big enough to afford him—which is only in the last six or seven years. My business wasn't big enough for that until recently. He only takes high-end clients and I wasn't high-end enough. I wouldn't have been high-end enough for him to take me then, but I did some PR work for him around the time he divorced his first wife. He wanted to hire another agency, but one of his other rich clients told him to use me instead. We got to know each other and he took me on "

"So…" She frowns. "You actually talk to him in person about your finances? You don't use one of his subordinates as an advisor?"

"No, it's him. We usually just chill out and shoot the breeze about my finances and what my goals are. It's friendly and informal because we know each other."

"That sounds nice. So what are your goals?"

That's as good a lead-in as I could possibly hope for. I pull a black velvet ring box out of my jacket pocket, crack it open, and set it on the table in front of her.

"I want to marry you. I told you before that I want to settle down and start a family. That's why I needed to rearrange my finances. I want to marry you and stop living together in sin the way we have been. I don't want to fool around. I want to make it official."

I mean it as a joke, but she doesn't hear me. She stares at the ring with her eyes hanging out of their sockets.

I tried to keep the ring subtle and understated but still elegant and stunning. I knew she wouldn't want something glaring and ostentatious.

"What do you think?" I ask. "Do you like it?"

She blinks at the ring once and then, without warning, she covers her face with her hands and bursts into a flood of tears.

"Baby?" I ask. "What's wrong? I love you. I never want to lose you."

She takes her hands down and doesn't stop crying when extends her hand to grab mine. "I love you! You're so sweet! I love you so much."

"Does that mean you'll marry me?"

"Yes!" she chokes. "Yes, I'll marry you."

I pick up the box and slip the ring on her finger. She smiles at me through her tears and squeezes my hand again.

Her father comes out of the kitchen just then, pops a bottle of champagne, and yells out when he raises it in one hand and two flutes in the other. "Hey! Tanta felicità!" He puts the flutes and bottle down and hugs us both before he starts pouring champagne for us.

Nicole looks back and forth between me and her father. "You....you knew about this, Papa?!" she gasps.

"Of course! He came to me three days ago and asked me to marry you. Eh?!" He clamps me hard on the shoulder. "My son! He said he wanted to surprise you and I should tell you to bring him here tonight." He slaps my cheek hard enough to hurt. "Such a romantic! He's a good boy! I like this one."

Nicole gapes at me. "You....you asked my father....for permission to marry me?"

"Sure," I tell her. "I had to."

She shakes her head and glances at her father. "Should I be worried about this?"

He bursts out in loud laughter, says something to her in Italian, and goes back to the kitchen. Nicole won't stop gaping at me. "This is nuts!" she husks.

"Why is it nuts? I figured your family was traditionalist that way and I wanted to make sure he approved. I asked him to help me surprise you and he loved it."

She lowers her gaze to the table and winds up looking at the ring. "This is crazy! I never thought anything like this would ever....."

She breaks off when we hear a crash coming from the kitchen. Her head shoots up and all the color drains from her cheeks. She knows this restaurant better than anyone. She knows a normal crash of her father working and when something is wrong.

She launches out of her chair fast enough to knock it over onto the floor. It slams down and she races away to the kitchen. I hustle after her and catch up with her just as she enters the kitchen.

"Papa!!" she yells. "PAPA!!"

She screams when she spots him lying on the floor between the hot line and the prep stations. He's ashen pale, sweaty, and unconscious.

She lunges for him, yanks him by the shoulders trying to sit him up, and his weight falls out of her hands. "PAPA!!"

I grab my phone and call 911. I'm on the line with the dispatcher trying to tell the woman the address when Nicole yells over her shoulder. "He isn't breathing!"

I almost drop my phone in my haste to go over there and check for myself. She's right.

She's already checking his pulse and she gives him mouth to mouth. She moves over to his chest to give him compressions, but I push her out of the way and start doing them one-handed myself while she keeps blowing air into his mouth.

I pant out the directions to the dispatcher. I have to ask Nicole for the address.

Her father doesn't revive. I don't let myself think about what will happen if he doesn't make it.

Nicole and I are still going full tilt doing CPR when the paramedics show up. I have to pull Nicole out of the way while they hook him up to their machines, shoot him full of drugs, intubate him, and take him away from us.

They leave me and Nicole standing there alone in the kitchen full of flickering burners, bubbling pots, humming ovens, and a million fluorescent lights shining everywhere.

I keep my arms around her as dead silence falls over the kitchen. This is the worst disaster yet—and we don't even know if her father will make it. He better. She needs him. In a way, she needs him more than she needs me.

I don't want to think about any of that. "Let's shut this place down and go to the hospital," I tell her.

She pulls out of my arms. She won't look at me. She goes through the restaurant in a numb trance turning off all the burners and ovens and putting all the food away.

She works silently and mechanically. She's been doing this almost her whole life. She doesn't leave even one scrap of food lying out.

I half expect her to clean up all the dishes, too. I wouldn't be surprised, but she doesn't. She leaves everything in the sink and I drive her to the hospital.

Chapter 32: Rory

Nicole and I go into the hospital emergency room and check in with the triage nurse. "We're looking for Vitale Gerace," I tell the nurse. "He just came in by ambulance a little while ago."

"Take a seat over there," she tells us. "I'll call upstairs and find out where he is."

Nicole and I sit down. She stares straight in front of her without responding to anything. She doesn't seem to be aware that she's wearing my engagement ring on her finger right now. I'm going to marry her. She won't be alone after this.

She's usually so energetic and lively about everything. Now she looks completely crushed. I get a very bad feeling when I see the way she's acting.

We wait an hour. No one comes to tell us what's going on with her father. The shift changes at the triage desk. That nurse leaves and a different lady takes her place.

I touch Nicole's arm and go over there to ask what's going on. "We're waiting to hear what's happening with Vitale Gerace," I tell the second nurse. "The nurse on the last shift was supposed to find out for us."

"Take a seat and I'll find out for you."

"That's what she said and we've been waiting an hour for any news. I would rather just wait while you check."

She makes a face and gets on her phone. I stand there in her face and block anyone else from coming forward until I get the answers I want.

She finally gets off the phone and looks up at me with a very different expression on her face. I know what she's going to say before she even opens her mouth. "I'm sorry. He didn't make it. He suffered a massive and sudden heart attack. There was nothing anyone could do."

I mumble, "Okay. Thanks," and step away from the desk.

Nicole sits across the room looking straight in front of her. She already knows. That's what this means. Some hidden part of her gut already knows. That's why she's so lifeless. No one has to tell her.

Maybe she suspected this when her father almost lost the restaurant. Maybe she always knew and believed in her heart that he would die on his feet in the kitchen—the place he most loved.

It was the most perfect time and place for him to die—when he was the happiest, when he knew his precious daughter had found a man who would take care of her and help her through this—when he no longer had anything to worry about.

Knowing she already knows gives me the courage I need to go over to her. I don't want to be the one to shatter her world, but I have to be. I don't want her to find out from anyone else.

I sit down next to her and she glances at me. Her eyes tell me loud and clear that she already knows. She knows exactly what I'm going to say the same way I knew what the nurse was going to say.

"I'm sorry, sweetheart," I murmur. "He's gone. He suffered a massive sudden heart attack. He didn't make it."

She turns her head to face front. She doesn't react. She just checks out and completely shuts down.

I wait a few minutes longer even though I know she won't come out of it. She won't shriek and cry and make a scene. She already knew. She knew the minute she found him in the kitchen.

Maybe she's always known it would end this way. Maybe she's been counting down the days before she walked into the restaurant and found him dead in his apron.

I go back to the triage desk and ask the nurse about making arrangements for the body.

She tells me I can basically do whatever the hell I want. The hospital has a policy to cooperate with the family's wishes as long as there are no extenuating circumstances that might require the Police Department to carry out an autopsy.

They obviously don't need to do that in this case, so I call one of the local funeral homes to come and get Vitale. I don't know what his kids will want to do with him.

I steer Nicole out of the hospital, put her in my car, and drive her home to our apartment. I park her on the couch and sit next to her while she stares at nothing for another hour or two. I don't try to talk to her. I don't want her paying attention to me right now.

I don't try to feed her dinner, either. I eventually take her upstairs, undress her, put her pajamas on her, and tuck her into bed. She doesn't acknowledge me even once through the whole ordeal. I really don't care.

I sit down on the edge of the bed next to her and press her thumb to her phone screen to unlock it. She doesn't make a sound or any facial expression while I navigate around and find the names of two men with the last name of Bates.

One of them is named Julian and has a New Jersey number. The other is named Stephen and has a California number.

I call them both, explain to them that I'm Nicole's fiancé, and that their father died tonight. I tell both of her brothers that I've arranged for a funeral home to pick up his body from the hospital, but that they could talk to Nicole about arrangements for the funeral.

They both thank me and tell me they're on the way right now. Stephen says he's going to get off the phone with me and start booking a flight out to New York. I tell him he and his family are welcome to stay with me and Nicole. We have room.

Julian tells me that he and his family will be staying at their own place in Jersey. He thanks me for my help and asks me how Nicole is. She doesn't show that she hears when I tell him she isn't doing too good.

I get off the phone with her brothers and keep an eye on her until she falls asleep. Then I change my clothes and slip out of the apartment.

I go down to the restaurant and stay up for the rest of the night washing all the dishes, cleaning the kitchen the rest of the way, and blowing out all the candles on all the tables. I don't want Nicole or her brothers to have to do it. I don't want them to do anything.

I get back to the apartment at sunrise just as she's waking up. She sits on the edge of the bed staring out the window at nothing.

I make her breakfast—a real breakfast—and she eats it in stunned, silent shock. She isn't home anymore and that's okay. I just have to be here.

I get a phone call from Stephen that his flight gets in at three that afternoon. He's been on the phone with Julian and they've been on the phone with the funeral home about doing the funeral the day after tomorrow.

Julian is the older brother and he's been on the phone calling all of the Geraces who still live in New York to tell them about the funeral. He also has a bunch of phone numbers for some of Vitale's old customers. Julian is spreading the word about the funeral.

He asks me to put Nicole on the line. I sit down next to her on the bed and hold out my phone. "Your brother wants to talk to you."

She takes it, holds it to her ear, and rasps, "Hello?"

She listens for a long time and then launches into a streaming torrent of Italian I can't understand. She talks loud and fast like she's angry. She doesn't cry.

She talks back and forth with her brother for a while before she hands back the phone. She turns away from me, lies back down on the bed, and pulls the covers over herself.

I put the phone back against my ear and say, "Hello?"

"She's satisfied with the arrangements we're making for the funeral," Julian tells me. "I guess I'll see you the day after tomorrow."

I thank him, tell him I'm picking up Stephen and his family from the airport later today, and we get off the phone.

I field a few more calls from the funeral home. They want to clarify that Julian and Stephen are empowered to make arrangements for Vitale's funeral. I tell them they are.

That's all I really need to do. I work on my devices while I hold down the fort and she stays in bed.

I talk to both brothers off and on up until Stephen gets on the plane to fly across the country. We talk about what to do about the restaurant.

I offer to contact the same broker Nicole was planning to use to buy everything in the restaurant. The brothers thank me and agree to let me handle it on their behalf.

I drive down to the restaurant and make several trips back and forth to take everything to my apartment. Vitale has a big chest freezer that I get a moving company to truck back to my apartment to store everything.

I ask her brothers if they want any of the food. They tell me to keep it. I make arrangements for the broker to pick up everything after the funeral. Then I contact the REIT board to tell them that Vitale is dead and his lease is canceled.

Julian wants to go with Nicole and Stephen to the restaurant and to their father's old apartment to divide up any old pictures, keepsakes, or his possessions that any of them want to keep.

I'm just getting ready to drive out to the airport when someone knocks on my door. I open it and find Hugo Bond frowning at me. "Is everything okay, Rory?" he asks. "I've been trying to get in touch with Nicole for hours. She doesn't answer her phone."

"Sorry, man. Her father died last night and she's a mess. She'll be out of action at least until the weekend. She has to get through the funeral and deal with all her father's possessions and stuff, so you guys will have to run the *Record* without her for at least a little while."

His features drain of all color. "Oh, my God! I'm so sorry! Tell her we're all thinking of her and tell her to take as much time as she needs. We got this. She doesn't have to worry."

"Thanks. I'll tell her."

I wait for him to leave, order a limo, and go pick up Stephen's family from the airport. My Beamer isn't big enough for all of them.

They make a big deal about the limo, but they're super nice and they all want to know when Nicole and I got engaged.

The story casts a shadow over everyone when I have to tell them that I'd just proposed to her a few minutes before her father collapsed and that we had to do CPR on him until the ambulance came.

I take them to my place. The apartment only has one guest room, so I give that one to Stephen and his wife. I arrange for his three kids to stay in the apartment across the hall. It's empty and they're all in their late teens. They need space they won't get at my place.

Stephen and his wife settle in and I start thinking about what to feed them for dinner. We have another day to get through before the funeral.

Stephen comes out of the guest room and intercepts me in the kitchen. He's a big guy carrying a lot of extra pounds. He looks almost as old as Vitale did and much heavier.

"I really appreciate you handling everything on this end," he tells me.

"No problem. I want you and your families to be able to concentrate on putting your father to rest. Whatever I can do, I will do."

His expression changes. "I would like to see my sister if you don't mind. I understand why you feel protective of her, but I really need to see that she's okay."

I don't tell him that she isn't. I don't tell him I'm not trying to protect her from him or anyone else she loves.

I open the bedroom door and see her sitting up on the edge of the bed in her pajamas. She's staring out the window again.

I take one look at her, make up my mind, and tell Stephen where she is. I don't stick around long enough to watch him walk into the room. He's about to find out just how not okay she is.

I go back to the kitchen and listen from a distance while he talks to her in Italian. She answers him clearly and politely enough. She doesn't break down crying. Did I really think she would?

He comes out of the room looking pale and horrified. "You okay?" I ask.

He passes his hand across his eyes. "I didn't realize it was this bad," he husks.

"Your father is all she's had for a long time. This was bound to hit her hard—and now the restaurant is gone, too. She depended on the restaurant as much as he did. It anchored her and gave her a sense of place. That's gone now. It will take her a while to rebuild that."

He stares at me in sinking horror. Then he turns away and shakes his head. "You know more about this family than I do. She's lucky to have you."

"I'm the one who's lucky to have her. I'll give her anything I can, but I can't give her that."

Chapter 33:
Nicole

I climb down the stairs and enter my father's restaurant. That time when we thought he was going to lose it—it prepared me for how deadly quiet the restaurant sounds now.

Nothing moves or bubbles or sizzles in the kitchen. All the tables and chairs have been stacked against the walls. The tablecloths, cutlery, candles, and vases lay in boxes in front of the tables.

Rory and my brothers have been working to get the restaurant ready for the brokers to come and get everything. Today will be the last time either my brothers or I will ever set foot in this place.

The three of us have just come from the funeral. Hundreds of people turned up to pay their respects to my father.

People I didn't know and had never even heard of got up to give speeches about how much he contributed to the community and how his restaurant offered a foundation of support, culture, and cama-raderie in Little Italy for decades.

Everyone cried at the funeral. Even my brothers cried, but I couldn't. I can't cry for my own father. I don't know why. He's just....gone. I don't know how to live or think or feel anything without him here. I don't even know how to understand it.

Rory has been the anchor for the whole family. He makes all the arrangements, drives everyone around in that rented limo of his, and stands aside while my brothers and I do whatever we need to do. He's always there.

I keep seeing the engagement ring on my finger. I'm going to marry him. I just don't know how to. I don't know how to love him or how to let him love me. I still love him more than anything. I'm beyond grateful for everything he's doing. I just don't know *how* to love him.

I know I should break out of this cold, frozen place I'm stuck in. I don't know how to do that, either. I talk to him or my brothers or anyone who wants to offer me their condolences on my father.

I'm a thousand miles away. I can't feel anything. I can't even kiss Rory or even look at him. I'm nothing. I'm nobody. I'm nowhere. I don't even exist.

My brothers keep telling me what a good man he is and how lucky I am to have him. They have no earthly idea. I know all of that, but I still can't break out of this place.

I haven't answered my phone in three days since my father died. I don't even know or care what's happening with the *Record*. The whole thing could have burned to the ground behind my back. I wouldn't know or care about that, either.

All of life seems a million miles away from me. The restaurant breathes with a thousand memories. They seep out of the walls.

My brother Julian starts sobbing the minute we walk in. My brothers have been a lot more demonstrative about their grief than I have. Everyone has been—which isn't saying much because I haven't been demonstrative at all.

Rory stands outside next to the limo right now and waits for my brothers and me to go through the restaurant and remove any personal effects we want to keep. I can't stand the sight of this place. The restaurant will never reopen. It will disappear along with my father.

Whatever my father accomplished with this business—however many lives he touched—that's all over and in the past now. I don't know if anything good will come out of this or if that chapter in history is lost now, too.

I pass through the kitchen to his office. Most of what's in here is business paperwork. Stephen comes in and we rummage through his desk. Then Stephen gets on the computer and starts going through the hard drive file by file.

I don't find anything I want to keep, so I go back outside and stand next to the limo with Rory while we wait for my brothers to finish.

Rory works on his phone during all the slow, dull periods of waiting for something to happen. There's been a lot of that since my father died.

Rory doesn't try to talk to me unless it's absolutely necessary. He doesn't touch me or put his arm around me or offer me any comfort. He just leaves me alone in my silence. That's what I need right now.

It's somehow so much more comforting to know that he understands. He knows I'm not okay and he lets me be not okay. He's by far the most understanding and relaxed about it of everyone.

My behavior horrifies my brothers, their wives, and all their kids. They all avoid me. I hear my brothers talking about me to Rory when they think I'm not listening. Neither of my brothers feels comfortable going home and leaving me like this.

Rory reassures them that I wouldn't want them to stay and that he doesn't know how long I'll be like this.

He tells them that they wouldn't be able to help me if they stayed and that he's fine with it if I stay like this for a long time.

He says he just wants to take care of me and make sure I have everything I need while I work my way through whatever I need to work my way through.

Julian and Stephen eventually come out of the restaurant with nothing. There's nothing personal in there that any of us wants.

Going to my father's apartment is a completely different story. I really don't want to go up there, but I have to.

Rory comes with us this time. I realize my mistake the minute I walk into the apartment. Family photographs, memorabilia, and tons of personal possessions crowd every single room.

My brothers start going through the place with a fine-toothed comb. They want to keep almost everything. They start discussing what each of them will take and talking about getting boxes to ship everything back to their own homes.

I come out of my parents' bedroom feeling sick. Rory sits on the couch working on his phone as usual. I can't look at him when I sit down next to him. He doesn't look up until I speak to him. "I need to leave," I mutter. "I want to go home."

"Okay. I'll take you. Just give me a sec." He stands up and goes into the bedroom. "Nicole wants to go home," he tells my brothers. "I'll take her there and bring you back some boxes."

They thank him. Neither of my brothers insists that I stay. They're getting the message.

Rory takes me back downstairs and we get into the limo. I should talk to him. I should tell him how I feel except that I don't feel anything. We go back to the apartment and I go to the bedroom. He hasn't tried to touch me since my father's death.

He hangs around just long enough for me to sit on the edge of the bed and stare out the window. Then he tells me he's going back to the apartment to help my brothers.

He doesn't come back until evening. He brings Stephen and Julian with him and comes into the bedroom and sits next to me. "Julian and his family are driving back to Jersey now," Rory tells me. "He wants to say goodbye to you."

I blunder out into the living room where Stephen and I say goodbye to Julian and his family. We all hug. They all tell me they love me. Those words me nothing to me right now.

Julian finally leaves and Rory orders food for the rest of us. He and Stephen talk late into the night. Stephen and his family are flying back to California tomorrow morning.

I can't even bring myself to stay in the same room to hear their conversation. I just want to be alone. I don't want to feel. I don't want to think. I don't want to be alive.

Chapter 34:
Nicole

R ory stops his car at the curb, sets the emergency brake, puts the car into neutral, and leaves the engine running with the heater on.

I glance out the window at the apartment building in front of us. "I don't even know why I'm here," I mumble.

"You're here because you believe in this project and that didn't change when your father died," he tells me. "You still believe in this project. You just hit a speed bump in the road. You'll get over this and your motivation will come back even if it hasn't come back yet."

"I'm glad you see it that way. I don't want to do this anymore."

"That's because you're inside it. You're in a dark place where the darkness is hiding everything bright and good outside it, but the brightness and goodness *is* outside it. You'll find it if you just keep going through the dark place until you get to the edge of it. Then you'll be able to see the world beyond it."

I can't look at him. I don't even have to ask how he knows that. I shouldn't be so down in the dumps over this—especially not when I'm sitting in the car next to him. I have nothing in the world to complain about.

I always knew my father would die. It's the natural order of things. People have children. The children grow up and the parents get old. The parents die and the children continue on.

"Do you want to know something weird?" I hear my voice talking from somewhere far away. It doesn't seem to belong to me anymore.

"What?" he asks. This is the first time I've talked to him since it happened.

"I realized I did all of this to make him proud of me. I didn't do any of it because I enjoyed it or believed in it or because I thought I could do some good in the world. I didn't do it because I thought it was important for someone to do it or even for the challenge of doing it well. It was all about him. I did it because he wanted me to. He wanted me to get a good job and contribute to society and he expected me to do well. It was never a question. It was what he expected and I did it. I never believed in any of it."

"Maybe you still can," he tells me. "Maybe you can still live up to his expectations even though he's gone. Maybe you can still try to make him proud by making a difference—or maybe it's time for you to come up with a new reason for doing all of this. None of that matters because you will come through the other side of this. You won't be like this forever. No one ever stays like this forever. Life has a way of bringing us back from anything no matter how bad it is. Life has a way of balancing the scales so we return to our equilibrium point. Staying out there in the dark is too unstable. It can't last and it won't last. If you don't want to go in there tonight, you don't have to. I'll take you home. You can take as long as you want to figure it out."

I heave a long sigh. "I guess I have to go. I can't keep doing nothing. I can't respect myself for acting like this."

"You're the only one who thinks so. No one thinks you're failing because you're grieving over your father. You can take as long as you need."

"Thanks, but I have to go." I lean across the seat and kiss him on the cheek. "I love you. I'll see you later."

"I love you, too. Call me if you need me, okay?"

I nod and he gets out of the car to open my door for me. He walks me up to the building entrance and we say goodbye before I go inside.

Things are returning to normal between us, but only on the outside. This impassable barrier still holds us apart. I haven't been able to be intimate with him since that night—the night he proposed to me.

I need to snap out of this. Every passing day impresses on me the urgency that I get my life back. I can't keep letting my father's death rob me of my happiness. Rory and I haven't even talked about setting a date. That isn't fair to him or to me.

I go into the building, ride the elevator to the fourth floor, and knock at one of the apartments. Hugo answers. His wife is just rounding up the kids to go put them to bed.

The rest of the co-op members are already here. We settle down on the couches in the living room for our weekly strategy meeting.

We start off by talking about the business, how everything is going, and any changes we think we need to make. This is the first time I've come to one of these meetings since my father died. I can't get interested in any of this.

I can't get interested in any of the stories the others are floating for our publication. The Easterman Senate campaign is becoming explosive.

Brody has been running a massive exposé on three sexual harassment complaints lodged against Easterman during his time as a regular cop before he got promoted to Deputy Chief of Police.

None of this interests me at all. I shouldn't even be here. The others ask me about what I want to get involved in. I talk about the Spiderware story and how it connects to a few other military contracts we've been finding out about lately.

We talk about running the story of Demetrius Runyon's murder conviction and we decide to see if any of our readers can give us any clues about how Spiderware may have leaked into other illegal military contracts overseas.

I agree to interview Diego about it and see if his contacts in Europe can shed any light on this, but I still don't feel any connection to any of this. I'm just going through the motions.

I don't want to let my colleagues down. I was the one who spearheaded the development of this cooperative. It wouldn't fall apart without me. The others are energetic and committed enough to keep the *Record* going.

I guess that's the problem. We agreed that we wouldn't let anyone be a part of this co-op if they weren't fully committed, engaged, and enthusiastic about the mission. That used to be me. Now I'm not. I don't even belong in the same room with these people.

The meeting goes on for a long time. I eventually can't stand it a second longer. I text Rory to come and pick me up. I meet him on the curb outside, get into the car, and we drive home in silence.

I slump on the couch and stare down at my hands. "I just can't do this anymore," I mumble. "I'll only drag them down."

He doesn't answer. He's just there.

He won't care if I quit the *Record*. He doesn't care if I ever work another day in my life. He'll love me the same way no matter what.

All of those things are superficial to the way he feels about me. No one knows better than he does how much my father and the restaurant meant to me. Now they're gone and I'm left rudderless on the ocean.

Rory doesn't try to fix it. He just lets me be wherever I need to be. He didn't fall in love with me because of my job.

We eventually go to bed together. I put my arms around him, but I already know we won't do anything. Is that part of your life together dead now, too?

I shouldn't even be walking around wearing his engagement ring if I can't give him all that I am. I don't want half a marriage. I don't want him to go without. He should have a woman who loves him completely and is engaged and loving toward him. I'm not.

Holding him like this feels like such a violation. It's unfair to him for me to pretend I feel something when I don't. I don't want to lie here and let him do it to me if I don't feel anything for him. I couldn't do that to him.

I pull away and roll onto my back. I want to roll onto my side and turn my back on him, but I can't do that. I wince when I realize how badly I'm rejecting him.

The thought of touching him makes my skin crawl. How can I even stay in this apartment with him when I feel like this?

He rolls on his side facing me. He doesn't demand that I do anything I'm not ready for. He just lies there facing me and waiting for me to come back to him.

He would welcome me with open arms if I wanted him. He would hold me like that all night with no expectations at all.

He's the one who loves me. I can't even claim to love him anymore because I'm not loving him. I'm not doing the actions of loving him. I'm not showing him that I love him and making him feel that I do.

I lie awake staring at the ceiling until he finally falls asleep. Then I roll onto my other side and face the other way. He would sleep with his arms around me from behind if I let him.

I fall asleep like that and wake up alone the next morning. He's already gone to work. Now I have to face the whole day alone in this apartment. I should just move out. I should let him move on and find someone else—someone who is a suitable partner for him.

Those words slap me in the face. He was so worried that I wouldn't find him suitable. Little did he know I would be the one to let the whole team down. He didn't know I would be the one who failed him instead of the other way around.

I go to the kitchen to eat breakfast. I don't care what I eat. I don't care about eating at all. I don't see the point in any of this.

I slump on the couch and look out the windows at the park. All those people have somewhere to be and something to do. They have families. They have jobs. They have responsibilities. I don't have anything.

Why do I even stay? Why am I in this apartment pretending to be engaged to Rory? Why am I even still involved with the *Record* when I don't care about it anymore? What's the point of any of this?

I'm still sitting there trying to figure it out when someone knocks on the apartment door. It better not be a salesman or some religious evangelist. I might have to go postal on somebody if it is.

I yank the door and freeze when I see Melody Gottlieb, Paige Novak, Emberlynn Rhinehart, Samantha Mulholland, and Vivian Salazar standing in the hall.

I realize in a moment of pure horror that I'm standing in front of them in my pajamas. My hair is a mess and I'm not wearing any makeup. I look like something the cat dragged in.

None of them even glances at my pajamas or my hair. They all smile at me. "Hi," Vivian greets me. "Do you mind if we come in and talk for a while?"

"Uh....what are you doing here?" I narrow my eyes at them. "Did Rory tell you to come and see me?"

"Rory?!" Samantha exclaims. "He doesn't know we're here. That's why we're here. We wanted to see you when he isn't around."

"Well, he isn't around." It takes me a minute to fully understand that they aren't here to see him. "Is something wrong?"

"We just want to talk to you," Emberlynn tells me. "We know you're having a rough time since your father died. We want to offer you our support."

"I don't need any support." I really want to slam the door in their faces. "I just want to be left alone."

"Then how about if we come in and talk at you? You don't have to do anything except sit there. Then we'll leave. Okay?"

"What do you want to talk about?" I hear the demanding, defensive tone in my voice, but they all pretend it isn't there.

"Business," Emberlynn tells me. "We want to talk about business."

"I'm not in business—not anymore. I'm actually planning on stepping away from the *Record*. I'm not as committed to it as I need to be. The co-op has a standard to maintain and I'm not maintaining it."

"That's what we want to talk to you about," Melody replies. "If you aren't too busy."

I wince at those words. I'm not busy. I'm not doing anything. I'm just sitting around feeling sorry for myself.

I walk away into the living room and buckle onto the couch where I was before. I don't even have the gumption to invite these women inside or offer them hospitality. I really want them to leave.

They come inside anyway—God only knows why. I don't see what I could possibly tell them about business. They've forgotten more about business between them than I could ever learn in a lifetime.

They settle around the circular living room. Some cross their legs. Others tuck one leg underneath them.

Emberlynn goes over to the windows and looks out at the traffic along Central Park West and the trees across the street. "This apartment is so cool! It isn't as big as some of the others, but that's what makes it so charming, doesn't it?"

I do my best not to make a face at her. They aren't here to talk about how cool the apartment is. The apartment wouldn't be enough to make me stay with Rory.

He would be crushed if I left. That would suck for him.

"Anyway," Samantha begins. "We all understand about your father dying...."

I snort in her face. "Something tells me you don't."

"You aren't the only person who has suffered tragedy in your life, you know," Melody tells me. "You aren't the only person who has lost a loved one or even lost everything in your life in one split second. Some of us have gone through the same thing. We aren't here to tell you to stop being broken and beaten down by that. That's what Samantha is saying. We actually do understand it because some of us have gone through exactly the same thing."

I look away. I would rather pretend that I don't know what she means, but I can't pretend that. She lost a hell of a lot more than I did. She lost her father under much worse circumstances. She lost everything—her whole family—everything—in a split second.

"The real reason we're here, Nicole," Paige tells me, "is because we're worried."

"You don't have to worry about me," I mutter out the side of my mouth. "I'll get over this eventually."

"We aren't worried about you," Vivian corrects. "We're worried about ourselves—and each other."

My head whips around. "What?! Why are you worried about yourselves?! You're married to billionaires! Melody and Paige *are* billionaires. You have nothing in the world to worry about."

"We have all of that *now*," Emberlynn points out. "But we could lose it all in a heartbeat."

"Everything we have we got through hard work," she tells me. "Each of us built our careers from nothing. Melody inherited her fortune from her father, but he built that fortune through hard work. None of us got here because anyone gave it to us. You must understand that because Rory is the same way."

"So?" I counter. "That just proves that you deserve the money you have. You deserve all the success."

"But you're one of the very few who sees it that way," Samantha points out. "There are still people out there who hate The Billionaires' Club just because its members have money. Those people don't understand how the members got their money. Those people don't care that Lane grew up in a tenement in Harlem or that Rory grew up abused and living in a dumpster. Those people want to take the members' success away from them for no reason. How is that fair?"

"And if someone could do that to a member of the club, they would do it to any of us," Vivian points out. "No one is safe. I'm not a billionaire. My business is just getting off the ground, but what is there to stop someone from coming after me just because I have some money? What if I get successful and the same people decide that I'm one of the evil monsters because my business succeeded?"

"Someone could do the same thing to the *Record*, too, you know," Emberlynn points out. "The *Record* is doing well right now. It's doing well because all of you have put in the time, effort, and commitment to make it work. What if one of these people decides you shouldn't be succeeding at all because you made some money at it that they didn't—or couldn't? Then these people would go after you, too. They would go after anyone."

"That's why we need you, Nicole," Samantha tells me. "The world needs you and the world needs the *Record*. That's why the guys invested in you, because of your integrity to the story. The readers need that from you. The whole world needs that from you."

"Your father would be extremely proud of what you've accomplished," Melody finishes. "He never would have guessed you could come as far as you have—and this is just the beginning. You can become something so much greater. You would be doing him a disservice and seriously letting him down if you threw away all the good you could do in the world just because he died." She grimaces at me. "Believe me, there is not a day that goes by when I don't have to remind myself of that. I want to give up every day, but I keep going because I know how disappointed he would be if I quit." She sniffs. "He's been gone for almost four years and I still feel him watching over me. He never raised me to be a businesswoman, but I know he would be incredibly proud if he could see me now."

Samantha puts her arm around Melody's shoulders and hugs her.

"You seem to think we're all doing this because we want to and because we like it," Paige goes on. "The truth is that none of us wants to and we don't like it. We do it because we have to. We do it because the world needs us. There are people out there suffering from incurable medical conditions who can only survive because of the equipment my company supplies. There are countless people working for each of us who depend on us for their livelihoods and so they can support their families. We do this because the world needs our contribution—and the world needs you, too. None of this works if you quit. The world doesn't work if everybody quits. If you don't do it, someone else has to do it for you. That isn't fair. We know you wouldn't stand by and let something like that happen. We know you better than that. That is n't you."

I can't look at any of them. I turn my head and wind up looking at the same view. That's what I'm doing. I'm letting my father down. I'm letting myself down. I'm letting Rory down. I'm letting the whole world down.

I'm doing one worse. I'm letting these women down. I'm letting everyone in the club down.

Why did I even bother to defend the club if I'm just going to leave these people to the whims of fate? I might as well have saved my breath. Defending them once means nothing. They're right. Someone else could come along tomorrow and do exactly the same thing.

I don't want to believe I would just pull the covers over my head and let it happen, but that's exactly what I am doing. That's exactly what I would be doing if I walked away from the *Record* now—or ever.

I would be leaving Rory to the whims of fate right along with the rest of the club. Someone could go after him just because he has money. The person might even know about his background and all the terrible conditions he had to overcome to get where he is.

The person might not even care that he worked hard to earn his money or that Diego gives most of his wealth away to people who need it.

These unscrupulous people might just want to lynch him for no good reason—just because they have some vendetta against The Billionaires' Club.

Cain Palmer has more money than he knows what to do with and he went after The Billionaires' Club. The person he hated isn't even alive anymore. These people are totally irrational and insensible to the facts.

Plenty of good people do still care about the facts. They've been pounding down my door ever since I took on the *Record* and made it into something better. People need this.

I wouldn't be making the world a better place by quitting. I would be making the world a worse place. I would be letting the bad guys win. I can't do that.

I mumble something about how these women have given me a lot to think about. I thank them for coming and stop short of actually kicking them out of the apartment.

I can't keep sitting around. I'll always carry the burden of my father's death, but Melody is right. He would be absolutely sickened if he thought I had the power to make the world a better place and didn't use it. He would never tolerate that.

I go back to the bedroom, take a shower, and change into my real clothes. I don't know where I'm going, but I have to get out of here. I've been locking myself away for over two weeks. That's long enough.

I go downtown and wind up at the New York City public library. I always liked coming here to do research.

I go inside and start searching the stacks. Then I get an idea, sit down at one of the tables, and pull out my phone.

First I send a message to Diego Espinosa asking if I can interview him about his dealings with Demetrius Runyon. I assure Diego that I'm not after anyone in the club and that I'm actually interested in getting his help in some of my wider investigations.

He's extremely warm and inviting about it and we set a time for next week. Then I look up a few of the names Brody dropped on the Easterman investigation.

My blood runs cold and I practically choke when I recognize the names of the women who accused him of sexual harassment. All three of them work for organized crime syndicates in New York.

This is turning into something bigger and more convoluted than any of us ever suspected. Did the New York mob have something on Easterman—or was he one of them? Did the syndicates put Easterman up to framing Diego?

I hustle out of the library and walk all the way back to the apartment. It takes a long time because I keep stopping in my tracks to make phone calls and look things up on the internet. I have a million things to do and not enough hours in the day to do them.

The darkness fades out in a heartbeat. I can see the world of brightness and goodness beyond the shadowy fringes. That world needs me. It needs me real bad and I don't have a moment to spare before I get back to work.

I make it back to the apartment after five. Rory looks up from the kitchen counter where he sits there working on his computer.

"Where you been?" he asks. "I didn't know you left. I was just wondering if I should be getting worried."

"Sorry. I should have texted you that I was going out. I won't make that mistake again."

He stares at me. We haven't texted since my father died. He doesn't disturb me and I don't disturb him. We lead separate lives.

That stops now. All of it stops now.

"I had to do some research for one of the stories the *Record* is working on," I tell him. "And I'm meeting with Diego next week to talk about Spiderware."

He raises his eyebrows. "Uh....okay. Are you okay? Did someone set off a firecracker under your ass?"

I laugh. "You could say that—but listen. I need to talk to you about something."

"Fire away. I'm all ears."

I walk over to him, pull his stool sideways so he isn't sitting right in front of the counter, put my arms around his neck, and climb onto his lap so I'm straddling him.

He glares at me. This is the first time we've gotten close since that night—the night we got engaged.

"Is this what you wanted to talk to me about?" he snarls.

"Actually...." I ride him harder and feel his body charge with energy. "Actually I think it's long past time we talked about setting a date for the wedding."

He grabs my hips and grinds me down on his hard package. "What wedding?"

"The wedding where we vow to love, honor, and cherish each other until death do we part."

He dives into my neck and bites me hard. I scream and start to struggle in his powerful arms, but he knows better than to think I'm trying to get away.

"I made that vow a long time ago, baby," he growls in my ear.

I wrestle my way out of his arms and grab his tie to pull it off. His smoldering eyes make me ache to rip his clothes open and devour his body in big greedy mouthfuls. "You did...." I pant. "Now you need to hear me say the words."

"You're wearing my ring." He pumps between my legs again. "Did you think you were going to get away from me?"

I scream as another wave of brutal delirium sweeps over me. I'm gasping and moaning too much to answer.

His hands close around my ass and guide me into a steady, pounding rhythm. There's no escape and I don't want there to be. I'm free from the darkness. Now nothing can stop me from embracing this man that I love so much.

Nothing will stop us from making all our dreams come true. He already makes mine come true just as I make his come true. Neither of us will stop until we make it a reality.

The End.

Keep Reading

Firehouse Blues Series

You can find it at your favorite book retailer.

Get All of AE Moran's Free Books

S ign Up Once—Get all A.E. Moran's free books including brand new releases

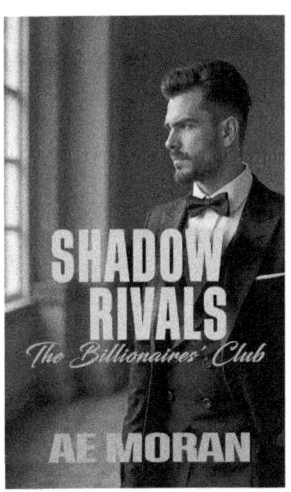

Holden Seager is hot, magnetic, and filthy, stinking, obscenely rich. He commands a room the minute he walks in the door. So what happens when meets another shark as powerful, as charismatic, and as successful as he is—not to mention ten years younger? When these two meet across the negotiating table, one of them will walk away the undisputed winner. The other will walk away with nothing.

Or so it seems.

Unless they're best friends.

When the business deal of a lifetime falls flat on its face and neither of these titans knows how to bring it back to life, this might be the opportunity Dayna Turner has been waiting for.

There's just one problem. She works as an assistant to one of these powerful men....and she's in love with the other. It's a recipe for disaster and heartbreak—unless Dayna can pull off an even bigger coup that will leave them all richer, happier, and more closely connected than ever. The alternative is the destruction of everything all three of them have worked so hard to build.

Sign up at www.authoraemoran.com to read it for free.

About AE Moran

A.E Moran is the contemporary romance pen name for Theo Mann.

I write 70 books per year—and yes, before you ask, all these books are my original creative work. Nothing written under my name is AI-generated or ghostwritten because I write better than AI and any ghostwriter out there.

People don't read fiction for entertainment or to escape from reality. People read fiction to see their humanity reflected in another person's character and story.

This is my promise to you. When you read my books, you'll see your own humanity reflected in the characters and stories. I take this commitment to my readers very seriously. My books are an intimate form of communication between us. I would never disrespect my readers by turning that over to a machine or another writer. This is my bond between me and you as my reader.

I write 20,000 words per day as my daily work output. If anyone with a public platform would like to challenge me to prove this in a controlled environment, feel free to contact me on this website's contact page.

I worked as a professional ghostwriter for fifteen years. Now I'm going for the Guinness World Record by writing 700 books over the next ten years and 1400 books over the next twenty years, all originally written by me. See my website for the full book list.

I'm also the author of *Proof for the Existence of God* and the *Crimes Against Fiction* blog. You can find all my nonfiction work at www.crimes-against-fiction.com.

If you have a story idea, or if you would like me to explore a series in more depth, or if you'd like me to explore a character by writing a spinoff series about that character or world, leave me a message on my website's contact page. I answer all reader emails, so ask me anything, tell me what you liked and didn't like, and let me know where you'd like your favorite series to go. I would love to hear your ideas and find out what you'd like to read next.

You can find out more at www.theomann.com or at www.authoraemoran.com.

Also by AE Moran (so far)

Standalone Novels

Heart on a Knife Edge

Dream Dimension

Just Friends

Back From the Dead

Damaged

Small Town Reunion

Series

Firehouse Blues (Books 1-10)

Turning Point Ranch (Books 1-10)

The Billionaires' Club (Books 1-10)

Paradise Cruises (Book 1-8)

Royal House (1-10)

Summerton Estates (1-10)

www.ingramcontent.com/pod-product-compliance
Lightning Source LLC
Chambersburg PA
CBHW052021020726
47501CB00004B/1179